CLOCKWORK HEARTS

A TIMELESS AFFAIR

LILLIANA ROSE

BLURB

Time is fragile. I never expected it to shatter—and take me with it. Everything changed the day I opened a package containing a glowing pendant that shouldn't have existed. The world shifted, and I fell through time itself.

Now, I'm stranded in a past where the line between science and magic blurs, and the man with the mechanical heart—Thaddeus—holds the key to both.

He has built the chronarium, which is connected with power and time. It could be my only way home, but I'm not the only one who wants it.

I might never return to my time—or the life I thought I wanted. But in this fractured world, I've found something unexpected—a cause worth fighting for and a man worth risking everything to save.

Time is running out.

But if I've learned one thing, it's that even monsters can fight for the future.

CHAPTER 1

$\mathcal{E}$velyn

The fluorescent lights of the museum archives hummed a discordant buzz against the whispers of the past that echoed in my mind. I ran a gloved hand over a Victorian ledger, its cracked leather binding whispering stories of forgotten lives—lives I envied, lives lived in a world of gaslight and shadows, a world I longed to escape to.

The scent of aged paper, usually a comfort, today felt suffocating, a reminder of the dust and shadows that had become my world. My colleagues, even the fellow introverts who sought refuge in the quiet corners of the museum, steered clear of this particular collection—boxes upon boxes of Victorian ephemera, deemed too mundane, too poorly documented, to warrant their attention. Too... ordinary.

But I had a deadline. And this dusty, forgotten collection, I desperately hoped held the key to meeting it. More than that, it held the key to my future, to finally escaping the suffocating weight of academic obscurity.

Lately, the whispers of the past had taken on a new edge, a subtle warning I couldn't quite decipher. A sense of unease as if the ghosts weren't entirely content to remain silent observers.

The museum director, Mr. Perkins, a man whose ambition outweighed his appreciation for historical accuracy, had given me an ultimatum to produce a publishable paper on some aspect of the Victorian era by the end of the month, or my research grant, the lifeblood of my long-gestating doctoral thesis, would be terminated.

Years of painstaking research poring over dusty documents and forgotten artifacts would all be for nothing. The pressure had been a constant, throbbing ache in my chest, a weight heavier than any stack of Victorian ledgers. If I failed, my dreams of a life dedicated to unraveling the mysteries of the past would crumble to dust.

"Victorian bits and bobs, Evelyn," Mr. Perkins

had said earlier as he unceremoniously dumped the boxes on my table. "Think of it as a treasure hunt!" His wink, meant to be encouraging, sent an involuntary shiver down my spine. I preferred my treasures inanimate and undisturbed, thank you very much.

Pulling on my gloves, the familiar sense of unease intensified, prickling my skin like a thousand tiny needles. It was more than just the pressure of the deadline, it was a deeper, more primal fear, a sensation I often experienced when handling objects imbued with the energy of past lives. It was as if something, or someone, was watching, waiting for me to unearth their secrets. Waiting to claim them. I hesitated, a sudden chill settling over me despite the warmth of the archives. I shook it off, telling myself it was just nerves.

I opened the first box, its wooden sides warped and cracked with age, releasing a faint scent of decay and something else. Something metallic and sharp, like ozone before a storm—tarnished lockets, mourning jewelry heavy with jems, dried flowers brittle as autumn leaves. Each piece is a whisper of a forgotten story, a fleeting glimpse into a life lived and lost. Beautiful, yes, but nothing groundbreaking that would save my thesis. Nothing that would silence the whispers or the growing sense of dread that coiled in my stomach.

Then, I saw it. Tucked away in a corner of the box, almost hidden beneath a tangle of faded silk ribbons, a small, ornate pendant. Unlike the other jewelry, it wasn't silver but darker and heavier. Almost onyx. It was circular, crafted in the shape of a clock face, the hands frozen at half past three. Half past three. What significance did that time hold? A shiver ran down my spine. Beneath a crystal dome, intricate gears and tiny levers whirred and clicked, humming with almost imperceptible energy that vibrated against my skin, a faint, rhythmic pulse, like a heartbeat, even before I touched it. My breath hitched. I checked the inventory list, my heart quickening with a sudden surge of excitement. It wasn't there. Unlisted. Undocumented. Intriguing. This could be it. The unique find, the missing piece, the key to unlocking my research, saving my thesis, silencing the whispers, and escaping the shadows.

A strange compulsion, a pull I couldn't explain, a whisper on the wind of time, a siren's call from the depths of the past, drew me to it. My methodical nature, usually so dominant, evaporated like morning mist, and I removed my glove. I had to touch it. I reached out, my fingers trembling as I brushed against the cold, unfamiliar metal. The moment my skin made contact, a jolt, sharp and electric, shot through me, followed by a wave of dizziness so intense the room swayed around me. I gasped, my breath catching in my throat. The fluorescent lights above flickered violently, the humming escalating to a high-pitched whine, and the room tilted, the shelves of books and artifacts blurring into a dizzying, disorienting kaleidoscope. The metallic scent intensified, filling the air, thick and cloying, making my head spin.

The whispers of the past, once a comfort, now rose to a deafening roar, swirling around me, pulling me in, promising secrets and mysteries, dangers and delights. My skin prickled with a strange energy, a thrilling, terrifying anticipation of the unknown. The whispers intensified, becoming a cacophony of voices—near and far, past and present—crashing over me, pulling me under, drowning me in the echoes of time.

CHAPTER 2

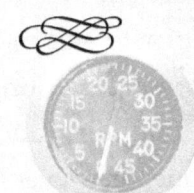

$\mathcal{E}$velyn

I blinked, trying to focus, but the world swam in a hazy blur, and my head ached. Cobblestones, rough and uneven, pressed against my cheek, their coldness a shock against my skin. The metallic tang lingered, acrid and unsettling, like the breath of something unnatural.

I pushed myself up, my hand landing on something cold and slimy. I recoiled, my stomach churning. Where am I?

Slowly, the world resolved into a dimly lit alleyway, narrow and reeking of refuse. The stench made my eyes water. The sounds of the city, a mix of unfamiliar noises, assaulted my ears—the clatter of horses' hooves, the rumble of cartwheels, and shouts and laughter as I stumbled from the alley, blinking against the sudden, brutal sunlight.

The scene before me was overwhelming. Horse-drawn carriages, ornate and monstrous, rattled past, their drivers bellowing warnings I couldn't understand. Women in long skirts and bonnets and men in top hats stared at me, their eyes lingering on my jeans and T-shirt, their whispers like the buzzing of insects.

I felt exposed, vulnerable, like a butterfly pinned under glass. The air was thick with coal smoke, the stench of horse manure clinging to the back of my throat, and beneath it all, that persistent metallic tang, a subtle, sinister undercurrent that made my skin crawl. It was as if someone was watching me, tracking my every move.

Panic clawed at me. I fumbled for my phone, my lifeline to a world that suddenly felt a million miles away. No signal. My sleek, modern watch had stopped at three thirty—the same time as the pendant. The thought sent a fresh wave of dizziness through me.

Time travel. Impossible. Insane. Real.

Tears pricked my eyes. I wanted to go home, a desperate plea against the rising tide of fear. I needed familiarity, an anchor in this alien world. Stranded in when?

Judging by the clothes, the carriages, and the stench of horse manure, sometime in the 19th century. But how?

The pendant, I hung it around my neck. The strange clockwork pendant had to be the key. Nausea washed over me. I needed to find something familiar, an anchor in this swirling vortex of the past.

The museum. My sanctuary. It had to still be here. Surely, some things remained constant across time.

Driven by this desperate hope, I started walking, my modern shoes slipping on the uneven cobblestones. The streets were a labyrinth, a confusing maze of narrow lanes and imposing buildings. I asked for directions, my modern accent eliciting curious stares and hesitant responses. After what felt like an eternity, I finally arrived where the museum should have been.

My heart sank. Instead of the imposing modern structure I knew, a smaller, older building stood in its place, its brick façade blackened with soot, its windows dark and uninviting. A brass plaque identified it as the "London Institution," a name that meant nothing to me. This wasn't my museum. This wasn't my time.

Just as despair threatened to engulf me, a figure walked past, unlike any I'd seen before. Tall and imposing, dressed in a finely tailored suit, it moved with a strange, stiff precision. Its skin was unusually pale, its eyes an unnervingly bright blue, and as it turned, I glimpsed a flash of metal beneath its starched collar.

An automaton. A lifelike, functioning automaton.

My breath hitched. Then, another passed, carrying a heavy trunk with effortless ease, its movements as smooth and silent as a well-oiled machine. And another, polishing the brass doorknob of a nearby shop, its face expressionless, its eyes fixed on its task. Servants. Automatons as servants. This wasn't just a different time but a different reality.

The realization sent a shiver down my spine, a thrill of excitement mixed with a growing sense of unease. This world, this strange, unsettling world, held secrets I couldn't begin to comprehend. Secrets I suddenly, desperately wanted to uncover. But first, I needed to find my bearings. I needed to find a place to exist in this alien landscape. And perhaps, just perhaps, find a way back to my own time.

A woman dressed in a simple, dark gown emerged from the building, her brow furrowed as she looked at me. My jeans and T-shirt, while practical for navigating the dusty archives, were clearly not the fashion of this era.

"Are you all right, miss? You seem a bit... flustered." Her voice, though laced with concern, held a distinct note of suspicion.

"I'm... looking for the museum," I stammered, my voice trembling slightly. "The London Museum?" As I spoke, my gaze drifted to her hand, resting on the doorknob. It was different. Metallic. Intricate gears and levers whirred beneath a polished brass casing.

A mechanical hand. My pulse increased, unsure how to process this alternative world I was now in.

Her eyes, a startlingly bright blue, shimmered with an unnatural light. It was like looking into the heart of a finely crafted clock.

The woman followed my gaze, a wry smile twisting her lips. "Something catch your eye, miss?" she asked, her voice dry. She flexed her mechanical fingers, the gears whirring softly. "Don't see many automatons around here, do you?" Her blue eyes, unblinking, seemed to pierce through me, reading my thoughts. "What, did you just land here from another time or something?"

My heart hammered against my ribs. How did she... I opened my mouth to speak, but no words came out. "I-I," I stammered, my cheeks burning. "I'm just… lost."

"Lost? That's not a good thing to do in London, miss. You could end up with the wrong crowd before you take a breath." Her gaze was still fixed on me, unsettlingly intense. "Well, the London Museum is in Bloomsbury, miss. This is Finsbury Circus. Quite a ways off." She eyed my clothes with a mixture of curiosity and disdain. "And if you don't mind my saying so, you look like you've stepped out of a penny dreadful."

Bloomsbury. Finsbury Circus. The names swam in my head. Disorientated, I mumbled a thank you, my mind reeling, and turned away, my heart sinking. Lost. Utterly and completely lost in a world where mechanical women casually conversed about time travel.

The press of bodies around me was almost suffocating. I stumbled on the uneven cobblestones, my senses assaulted by the sheer number of people crammed into the narrowing street. Stares followed me, their gazes sharp on my out-of-place jeans and T-shirt. I felt like a specimen pinned under a microscope.

I'd dreamed of this, of walking these historic streets, of breathing the air of Victorian London. But the reality was overwhelming. Suffocating.

A speeding carriage, its driver bellowing, "Get out of the bloody road, you daft cow!" nearly took me out at the knees.

I yelped, stumbling back onto the grimy sidewalk, my heart hammering against my ribs. This wasn't the romantic, sepia-toned past I'd imagined. This was a world of dirt, danger, and difference. A world where I very clearly didn't belong.

Then, a flash of color caught my eye. A discarded newspaper on a bench, its headline proclaiming the wonders of "The Great Exhibition of the Works of Industry of All Nations."

The Crystal Palace.

A beacon of innovation, a testament to human ingenuity. A place where, perhaps, I might find a fleeting connection to my own time, a spark of recognition amidst the alien landscape. A glimmer of hope, however faint, flickered within me, a tiny ember in the gathering gloom.

I snatched up the paper, smoothing out the creases, my fingers tracing the bold, Victorian typeface. Hyde Park. I knew the name—a compass point in this disorienting temporal storm. With renewed purpose, I started walking, the shimmering promise of the Crystal Palace drawing me forward.

CHAPTER 3

$\mathcal{E}$velyn

As I approached the exhibition grounds, the crowds thickened, a mix of vibrant colors and excited chatter. The Crystal Palace itself, a magnificent glass and iron structure, rose before me from the manicured lawns of Hyde Park, breathtaking in its scale and grandeur.

I paused, momentarily mesmerized, a wave of something akin to wonder washing over me. This, at least, felt familiar—a celebration of innovation, progress, and a shared human experience that transcended time. The anchor I needed.

Sunlight streamed through its countless panes,

transforming the interior into a dazzling spectacle of light and shadow. Despite my disorientation, a sense of wonder bubbled up within me.

Inside, the palace was a labyrinth of exhibits. Gleaming steam engines hissed, intricate clocks ticked, and the air crackled with the magic of the telegraph. I felt eyes on me, a prickle of unease dancing across my skin.

I found myself drawn to a display near the center of the palace. Not the exhibit itself but the exhibitor. Tall and imposing, with an air of old-world elegance, he demonstrated a series of intricate clockwork automatons. But one particular invention held my attention—a small brass and copper device that pulsed with a faint, rhythmic light, almost like a heartbeat. Unlike anything else on display, its complexity and delicate craftsmanship far surpassed the other exhibits.

The clockmaker handled the device with a reverence that bordered on obsession. His movements were precise and economical, his gaze focused and unwavering. A low, resonant hum, like the whirring of intricate clockwork, emanated from him, a subtle vibration that seemed to resonate deep within my bones. He was undeniably captivating, something echoed with the strange energy of this altered past. As I leaned closer, I noticed a small, almost imper-

ceptible inscription engraved on the device's base—
Thaddeus Blackwood.

"Remarkable craftsmanship, Mr. Blackwood," I heard a man nearby murmur. "Truly a marvel of engineering."

Nearby, in a roped-off area, sat the Chronarium, a device of clockwork and crystal pulsating with a faint, inner light.

A nearby pamphlet detailed its history. A mysterious artifact unearthed by a renowned clockmaker, rumored to possess time-bending properties. I'd never believe this possible if I hadn't been hurtled back in time.

I scanned the pamphlet, noting the Chronarium was on loan to the Exhibition, a prized piece in this collection of human ingenuity. As I read, I saw Mr. Blackwood glance nervously toward the machine, a flicker of apprehension in his unusually bright blue eyes. He seemed more concerned with it than his own remarkable invention and the attention of other inventors in the crowd.

Suddenly, a commotion erupted. A group of figures cloaked in shadow moved with an unnatural, predatory grace. They were jarringly out of place amidst the celebratory atmosphere, their movements too precise, too synchronized.

One lingered near Blackwood's exhibit, his gaze

fixed not on the automatons but on the small, pulsating device. He subtly nodded to another before they moved toward the Chronarium. Before anyone could react, they disabled the security system and snatched the Chronarium.

As the crowd surged forward, gasps, confusion, and panic rippled between people. I noticed the thief with the Chronarium wasn't fleeing with the others. He had melted into the shadows near the back of the exhibit, moving with purpose to avoid the commotion.

Mr. Blackwood reacted instantly, his face hardening, his voice sharp and cold. "Retrieve it," he commanded. Beside him, a tall, imposing automaton, its metallic limbs gleaming, sprang into action.

A surge of adrenaline, sharp and hot, coursed through me. The Chronarium, a relic of the past, a potential key to understanding time itself, couldn't be allowed to fall into the wrong hands. Mr. Blackwood's reaction, his focused intensity, suggested more was at play.

What was so important about it? Was there something else they wanted?

Ignoring the voice of caution that whispered in the back of my mind, I followed, my gaze flitting between the fleeing thieves and the pursuing automaton. They moved with an unsettling swiftness, slipping through the throngs of people like shadows, their dark cloaks blending seamlessly with the shifting patterns of light and shade.

They led me out of the main hall and into a quieter, less crowded section of the palace, their pace quickening, their movements becoming more furtive, through a side exit and into a narrow, dimly lit alleyway. The air grew heavy, the metallic scent intensifying, mixing with the damp, musty odor of decay.

I saw one of the figures hand the Chronarium to another, who then melted into the shadows, disappearing with an unsettling swiftness as if he'd stepped through a hidden door, a rip in the fabric of reality. My skin prickled with a mixture of fear and excitement.

They'd wanted the Chronarium, but their focus was a carefully orchestrated performance. But for what? What was their true objective? And what did Blackwood have to do with it?

I turned to run, but it was too late.

The remaining figures blocked my path, their shadowy forms looming over me, radiating a menacing aura. The leader, his eyes glowing with an unnatural red, stepped forward.

"Well, well," he purred, his voice a low, predatory

growl. "What do we have here? A curious little stray, sniffing around where she doesn't belong." The metallic scent intensified, sharp and acrid, making my stomach churn.

My pulse quickened, fear coiling in my stomach. I opened my mouth to scream, but the sound died in my throat, choked by the rising tide of panic. His stench of uncleanliness intensified, making me gag. It wasn't just ale, it was something else. Something sharp, unnatural. Like the scent in the alley. I struggled against his grip, my mind racing, desperately searching for a way out.

"Give me the pendant," he growled at me.

"No way," I answered, then cringed. I unwittingly told him I had it.

The whispers of the past, once a comfort, now seemed to mock me, a chorus of forgotten screams echoing in my ears. This wasn't the past I had dreamed of.

Just as his hand reached for me, a sharp and commanding voice cut through the tension. "Leave her alone."

The figures turned, their eyes widening in surprise. Standing at the alleyway entrance, silhouetted against the faint glow of the Crystal Palace, was the clockmaker, his imposing figure radiating an aura of quiet power.

Even in the dim light, I recognized the pale skin, the unnervingly bright blue eyes, and the flash of metal beneath his collar. Beside him stood the automaton, its metallic limbs gleaming in the shadows. Its eyes were fixed on the thieves, its posture tense and ready for action.

"This doesn't concern you," the leader snarled, but there was a flicker of fear in his eyes, a hesitation that belied his bravado.

"You stole my invention. Of course, it concerns me," Blackwood replied, his voice a low, resonant hum like the whirring of intricate clockwork. His blue eyes, usually bright, now burned with a cold fire.

The leader lunged, a guttural roar escaping his lips, but Blackwood was ready. He moved with a speed that defied his size, intercepting the thief's attack with a clang of metal on metal. The fight exploded—a whirlwind of motion and brutal, metallic clashes.

The air crackled with the scent of ozone and hot copper, sparks showering down like angry fireflies as brass met steel. The whirring of gears within Blackwood intensified, a frantic counterpoint to the thieves' grunts and shouts.

They fought with a strange lack of commitment, their eyes constantly darting toward the alley's end as if expecting reinforcements—or perhaps a miracle. Bastion, the servant automaton, moved speed and precision. His polished brass limbs blurred in a dance of death and dismemberment.

One moment, a thief held a knife, the next, Bastion's hand had closed around his wrist, the gears whirring ominously as the thief screamed, the knife clattering to the cobblestones. With effortless ease, Bastion disarmed and disabled the remaining thieves, sending them scattering like rats fleeing a sinking ship. However, Blackwood remained focused, his gaze still fixed on where the other thief —the one with the pulsating device—had vanished.

Blackwood turned, his usually intense blue eyes softened with concern. "Are you all right?" he asked, his voice losing its metallic edge, a warmth replacing it that sent an unexpected shiver down my spine.

I stared, my heart pounding, mind racing. This automaton, this man? Relief? Gratitude? Something more? Dizziness washed over me.

"Sir, she looks like she's going to faint," the other automaton droned. As Blackwood reached out, his fingers brushed my arm. A sharp, electric jolt shot through me, making me gasp. His touch was strangely familiar yet unsettlingly charged. The metallic scent, acrid and coppery, intensified like blood on hot metal. The whispers of the past returned, a single chilling voice whispering my name.

This monster had saved me. And in that moment, our eyes met, a spark igniting between us—something inexplicable that transcended the strangeness, the danger, awakening the past.

CHAPTER 4

*T*haddeus

The alley reeked of ozone, copper, and decay. My gaze locked on the woman—this strange, alluring creature. Fear and *something else* flickered in her wide eyes. Fascination? She couldn't know what I was. A sliver of humanity might linger, buried beneath metal and clay, but I was more automaton than man, golem than human.

Her attire, jarringly modern, clung to her, revealing curves that sent a strange jolt through my circuits. Her sudden appearance—unsettling, inexplicable.

"Bastion..." I hummed, my voice a low resonance,

"... the Chronarium. Detain those responsible. The workshop." He inclined his head, a silent shadow melting into the deeper shadows of the alley.

She swayed, pale. As she faltered, I reached out, my metal fingers brushing her arm. An electric shock, alien and intense, shot through me. The air around her crackled, disrupting my automaton's gears, making the gas lamps flicker and cast grotesque shadows. Time itself seemed to warp. My internal clockwork stuttered—a sensation both unsettling and exhilarating.

She was chaos. A ripple in time. And yet, I was drawn to her. Where I'd touched her, her skin radiated a surprising warmth. *Desire.* A forbidden spark in my cold, mechanical core.

"Come," I murmured, the word unfamiliar on my tongue. I extended my hand, the metallic sheen catching the dim light. Hesitation warred with fear and desperation in her eyes.

"Who... who *are* you?" she whispered, her voice hoarse.

The truth—a patchwork of life and artifice, something that shouldn't be alive—felt impossible to say. "A friend, my name is Thaddeus," I answered. "You're safe now."

"Safe?" she echoed, disbelief heavy in her tone. Her legs trembled.

"Yes," I said, moving closer, each step calculated. "You need rest."

She flinched, glancing at the alley's mouth, but before she could flee, her eyes rolled back, and she collapsed.

"Easy," I whispered, catching her. Her fragility startled me. "Safe," I repeated, the word a vow. I cradled her close, the contrast of her feverish warmth against my cold metal stark and strangely compelling.

"I'm Evelyn," she murmured, her breath ghosting against my chest.

"Evelyn," I echoed, the name a whisper of discovery. I carried her into the street, her head resting against me, her breathing shallow. My workshop— my sanctuary—was the only place for her now.

Hailing a passing carriage, I settled her gently against the padded seat, adjusting her position and ensuring her comfort. As the carriage lurched forward, I studied her. She had delicate features, pale skin, and dark hair curling against her cheek. Fragile, yet with an underlying strength. I brushed a stray strand of hair from her face, my metal fingers trembling at the unexpected warmth of her skin.

A foreign, unsettling, yet compelling sensation. What was this pull she had on me? This inexplicable need to protect, to understand, to *feel*?

The carriage stopped outside my home. I carried her inside, the familiar ticking of clocks and hum of machinery a stark contrast to her stillness. Laying her on the makeshift bed, I watched her, questions swirling.

Who was she? Why *here*? Why *now*? And why did she awaken this warmth, this need, this flicker of life within me?

I covered her with a blanket, allowing myself one last glance before turning to my tools. Work to be done. Answers to find. But even as I focused on the familiar rhythms of my craft, she lingered—this strange, fragile creature who had upended my carefully ordered world. Her presence, a disruption, a chaos, and a terrifyingly alluring temptation.

CHAPTER 5

*T*haddeus

The tray of food hit the floor with a clatter, the sharp sound echoing through the workshop. Evelyn jerked awake, her wide eyes darting around the room, confusion etched into every line of her face. For a moment, she looked as though she might bolt, her body tense beneath the blanket I'd draped over her. Clara, meanwhile, already had her hands pressed to her mouth, her expression a picture of exaggerated horror.

"Oh, sir! I didn't realize you had company," Clara exclaimed, her voice rising in pitch. Her eyes darted to Evelyn, then back to me, her expression somewhere between scandalized and intrigued. "And a woman no less! My word, sir, what were you thinking?"

I sighed, pinching the bridge of my nose. "Don't be ridiculous, Clara. I found her. She needed help."

Clara let out a short huff, clearly unconvinced. She bustled over to Evelyn, her sharp gaze taking in every detail of the young woman as if inspecting a piece of silverware for tarnish. "Oh, miss, I frightened you tight and proper, so sorry for that, but... oh my goodness, what are you wearing?" She gestured dramatically at Evelyn's strange, fitted clothing, her expression a mix of horror and curiosity. "You can't go about like that! Scandalous, that's what it is. You'll have the neighbors talking. Mind you, there'll be talk enough already, what with the master bringing you here in the dead of night!"

Evelyn blinked at her, the color rising in her cheeks. She pulled the blanket tighter around her shoulders as though it might shield her from Clara's prying eyes. "I... I don't..." she stammered, her voice soft and hesitant.

"Clara," I said, more sharply than I intended. "Enough. She's been through a great deal. Leave her be."

Clara turned to me, her lips pursing into a thin line. "Well, someone has to look after her," she muttered, though she did step back, folding her arms over her chest. "Poor thing looks half-starved, and heaven knows what she's been through. Sit tight, miss. I'll fetch you something proper to wear and something edible."

With that, Clara swept out of the room, muttering about my lack of foresight as she went. I let out a frustrated sigh and turned back to Evelyn. She was still sitting stiffly on the cot, her gaze flitting around the workshop as though searching for some sort of anchor.

The room fell silent again, save for the rhythmic ticking of the clocks and the soft hum of machinery. The sound was one I had long since stopped noticing, but now, with her here, it felt louder somehow. More intrusive.

"This is my workshop," I said, breaking the silence. I gestured to the vast space around us, the towering shelves of tools and parts, the gears and cogs neatly sorted into labeled drawers. "A place of order amidst chaos. Everything you see here, every clock, every gear, every mechanism was built or repaired by my hands."

Evelyn's gaze followed my gesture, her wide eyes taking in the rows of ticking clocks, the brass orrery spinning slowly at the center of the room, and the faint glow of the gas lamps illuminating every detail.

Slowly, the tension in her shoulders eased, replaced by something else—curiosity perhaps or even awe.

"It's… incredible," she said softly, her voice laced with wonder. "I've never seen anything like it."

A faint smile tugged at the corners of my lips. "It's a comfort to me," I admitted. "The ticking of the clocks, the scent of oil and metal… it reminds me that some things in this world can still be predictable. Controlled."

She nodded slowly, though I could see the lingering apprehension in her posture and the way her fingers gripped the edge of the blanket. She was trying to mask her fear, her confusion, but I could see through it.

Her hand moved almost unconsciously to the pendant around her neck, a small, intricate clock encased in silver. It was strange, delicate, and yet oddly familiar. My gaze sharpened as I stepped closer, bending slightly to get a better look.

"May I?" I asked, gesturing toward the pendant.

She hesitated, her fingers tightening around the pendant for a moment before she nodded and lifted it to me, dropping it into my palm. I lifted the pendant gently, turning it over in my fingers. The clock face was elegant, the hands frozen at precisely three thirty. Something about it felt wrong. Or perhaps right, in a way I couldn't explain.

"It's stuck," I murmured, running my thumb over the glass. "Has it always been like this?"

"I... I don't know," she admitted, her brow furrowing.

As I held the pendant, a strange sensation rippled through me—a faint warmth, almost like a pulse, spreading from my fingertips to my chest. For a moment, the sound of the clocks around me seemed to fade, replaced by a low, steady hum. It was as though the pendant was alive in some strange way.

I released it quickly, stepping back as though it had burned me. The pulse subsided the instant it left my hand, but the memory of it lingered like the echo of a distant chime.

She noticed my reaction, her eyes narrowing slightly. "What is it?" she asked, her tone sharper now.

"Nothing," I said quickly, though the lie felt heavy on my tongue. "It's just... unusual."

She studied me for a moment, her gaze penetrating. "You're not like other men, are you?"

The question caught me off guard. I opened my mouth to respond, but the words wouldn't come. How could I explain what I was? A creature of clay and metal, held together by gears and something far less tangible. A being caught between worlds— neither fully human nor fully machine.

"I…" I hesitated, my gaze falling to my hand. The faint gleam of metal caught the light, a stark contrast to the flesh-like texture of my other arm. "It's… complicated."

"Complicated?" she repeated, her tone skeptical. "That's not much of an answer."

I met her gaze, unsure of what to say. Part of me wanted to tell her everything—to lay bare the truth of what I was. But another part of me, the part that had spent years hiding behind masks and half-truths held me back.

Finally, I said, "I'm not what you think I am."

She tilted her head, her expression softening slightly. "Then what are you?"

The question hung in the air, heavy and unanswerable. I turned away, moving to the workbench and picking up the glowing device I'd been dismantling earlier. My hands worked automatically, the familiar motions grounding me.

"I'm someone who can help you," I said at last, my voice quiet but firm. "That's all that matters right now."

She didn't respond, but I could feel her eyes on me, studying me. The silence stretched between us, broken only by the ticking of the clocks and the soft whir of the gears.

The pendant around her neck glinted in the light,

its frozen hands a reminder of the mysteries still to be solved. As I worked, my thoughts drifted to the Chronarium, the shadowy figures who had stolen it, and the strange connection I felt to this woman and her clock pendant.

Everything was connected, I could feel it. But the answers I sought seemed just out of reach, like the faint ticking of a clock in an empty room. And yet, despite the questions that plagued me, I found my attention drawn to her more than I cared to admit.

CHAPTER 6

*E*velyn

The silence between us became heavy and unrelenting. My breathing felt too loud, too out of place in the stillness of Thaddeus's workshop. The room around me ticked and hummed with a quiet, mechanical energy—alive yet cold.

I pulled the blanket tighter around my shoulders, trying to shake the lingering embarrassment from the maid's scandalized expression. The look she'd given me, as though I was some improper curiosity, crawled under my skin. But as I let my gaze drift across the workshop, the maid was quickly forgotten.

The space was overwhelming, a labyrinth of intricate chaos. Clocks of every size lined the walls, their faces frozen mid-tick, hands poised as though waiting for some unseen cue. Gears and mechanisms spilled from the surfaces of cluttered workbenches, their brass and steel glinting in the gaslight. A soft, rhythmic hum vibrated through the air as if the room itself was exhaling with the quiet power of its creations.

It was brilliant. And terrifying.

I shifted on the bed, the blanket brushing against the edge of the floor. Across the room, Thaddeus moved with precision, sorting through tools and parts with an efficiency that bordered on unnerving. He didn't speak or look at me, but I could feel his presence like a shadow at the edge of my vision. He was taller than I'd realized, his movements thought out and calculated as though his body were part of some grand mechanism.

Something about him felt off. Not in a bad way, but in a way that made my skin prickle and my instincts sharpen.

He wasn't like anyone I'd ever met.

I stared at him for a long moment, watching how the light caught on his features. His dark hair fell slightly over his brow as he worked, and his sharp cheekbones cast faint shadows across his pale skin.

He was handsome in a way that seemed almost too perfect—too measured.

And then there were the small details. The way his fingers moved over the parts on the workbench, quickly and precisely, like a machine assembling itself. The faintest gleam of metal was at the edge of his sleeve when he reached for a tool. A soft, rhythmic clicking sound, barely audible, when he shifted his weight.

What was he?

I shook my head and dropped my gaze to the floor as if looking at him too long might unravel something I wasn't ready to face. My thoughts drifted to how I'd ended up here—to the moment my life had shattered like glass.

The thief's face flashed in my mind, sharp and vivid. The memory of his voice, low and menacing, sent a shiver down my spine. "Give me the pendant."

I hadn't even known what he was talking about. All I knew was that I'd been cornered in a dark alley, my heart pounding and fear clawing at my throat. And then, before I could even scream, there was a flash of light, a rush of wind, and the world went wrong.

The pendant had done something to me. I didn't know why it had sent me hurtling through time, but I'd landed here in a world that didn't belong to me.

And now, the thief might still be out there. Hunting me.

I swallowed hard, brushing my fingers on the edge of the pendant around my neck. Its cold metal surface constantly reminded me of the questions I couldn't answer. It wasn't just the thief or my survival that scared me, it was the suffocating realization that I didn't know how to return to my time.

Would I ever see my world again?

Would I even survive long enough to try?

I glanced back at Thaddeus. He was my only anchor in this strange time, but I barely knew him. Could I trust him? He seemed kind in his own way, but there was a distance to him, an emotional wall I couldn't breach. And those small details—the gleam of metal, the rhythmic clicking—kept my guard up.

Still, what choice did I have?

Thaddeus turned, his sharp eyes briefly meeting mine and softening. "You should eat," he said, his voice low but steady. He gestured to a small plate of bread and cheese the maid had left behind.

I hesitated, then nodded, reaching for the plate. The food was plain but comforting, and the simple act of eating grounded me.

I watched him work for a while, studying the way his fingers moved over the delicate gears. The rhythmic clicking of his movements was almost hypnotic, but it also made my unease grow. Finally, I couldn't hold back the question any longer.

"What are you?"

Thaddeus froze, his hands stilling mid-motion. The quiet hum of the workshop seemed to grow louder in the silence that followed.

When he finally spoke, his voice was quiet, almost hesitant. "I told you. It's complicated."

"That's not an answer," I said, my tone firmer than I felt.

He turned to face me fully, his expression unreadable. For the first time, I noticed the faint lines of tension in his jaw, the way his shoulders seemed to carry a weight far heavier than the tools he worked with.

Finally, he sighed. "I suppose you deserve to know."

He raised his right arm, slowly pulling back his coat sleeve. My breath caught as the gaslight revealed the gleaming surface beneath—metal, polished and intricate, with joints that mimicked the movement of tendons and bone.

"I'm not... entirely human," he said, his voice steady but tinged with something I couldn't quite place. "My father... he saved me. After an accident. Using methods that most would consider unnatural."

I stared at the arm, unable to look away. "He built you?"

"In a way." Thaddeus lowered his arm, his gaze dropping to the floor. "He combined alchemical magic and mechanical engineering. Golem and automaton. He called it an experiment. I call it survival."

My stomach twisted, a mix of fear and pity swirling through me. "Why would he do that to you?"

"To save my life." His tone was matter-of-fact, but I could hear the pain buried beneath it. "I was born human, but I was attacked trying to save someone's life. This was the only way my father could save me."

I didn't know what to say. The revelation was more than I'd expected, but it also made him human in a way I hadn't anticipated. He wasn't just cold precision and sharp intelligence, he was a man who carried the weight of his survival like a curse.

"I'm sorry," I said softly.

Thaddeus looked at me, his expression unreadable. "You don't need to be."

For the first time, I saw a flicker of vulnerability in his eyes, and it made me feel braver. I reached for the pendant around my neck, holding it up so the light caught its surface.

"We're both a little out of sync with this world," I ventured.

He nodded slowly, his gaze intense. "You mean because you're clearly not from this era?"

I blinked, surprised. "You know?"

"I invented the Chronarium, Evelyn," he said, a hint of dry amusement in his voice. "Time travel isn't exactly a foreign concept to me."

The conversation shifted, the initial awkwardness replaced by a shared understanding. I told him about the thief, the device, the fear that clung to me like a second skin.

Thaddeus listened, his sharp mind piecing together the details. When I finished, he sat back, his expression thoughtful. "The Chronarium theft... the attack on you... they're connected. I can feel it."

"Connected how?"

"I don't know yet," he admitted. "But I intend to find out."

Looking at him then, I realized I didn't have much choice. He might be the only person who could help me.

"I'll work with you," I said quietly.

His lips curved into the faintest hint of a smile. "Good."

The silence lingered between us, broken only by

the faint hum of machinery. I could feel the weight of everything I'd learned—Thaddeus's nature, the connection between the thief of the Chronarium, and the fragile alliance forming between us. It was almost too much to process.

Before I could say anything else, the door creaked open, and the maid stepped back into the room. Her earlier flustered expression had been replaced by a look of brisk determination, though her gaze still flickered toward me with a trace of curiosity.

"I've laid out something more practical to wear," she announced.

Thaddeus straightened, brushing off his hands on his coat. "Thank you."

The maid sniffed, her tone sharp as she added, "So I'll be taking her to the main house now. She can't stay down here in... all this." She gestured vaguely at the workshop, her lips pursed in disapproval.

I glanced at Thaddeus, unsure whether to feel relieved or nervous. He hesitated, his gaze flicking between the maid and me as though weighing whether to argue.

Finally, he nodded. "Fine. But make sure she's comfortable."

The maid rolled her eyes. "It's not my first day, sir." She turned to me, her expression softening slightly. "Come along, miss. Let's get you cleaned up and settled."

I stood, clutching the blanket around me as I glanced once more at Thaddeus. His face was unreadable, though I thought I saw the faintest flicker of something—concern?—in his eyes.

"Thank you," I said quietly, unsure if I meant for the clothes, his help, or everything.

He gave a small nod. "We'll talk more later."

The maid ushered me toward the door, her hand light on my arm but insistent. As I stepped out of the workshop, the air seemed to change—warmer, softer, as though I'd left the pulse of a living machine behind. The hallway beyond was dimly lit, the faint smell of wood polish and candle wax replacing the metallic tang of oil and brass.

I glanced back once, catching a glimpse of Thaddeus standing in the doorway, his figure framed by the glow of the workshop. Then the door closed behind me, and he was gone.

The maid led me down the hall, her footsteps steady on the creaking floorboards. I clutched the bundle of clothes to my chest, my thoughts spinning. There was so much I didn't understand about this house, Thaddeus, or the device that had brought me here.

But one thing was clear—I wasn't alone in this anymore. For better or worse, I had someone on my side.

And I was going to need him.

CHAPTER 7

*E*velyn

After the mechanical order of Thaddeus's workshop, I'd half expected the rest of the property to look like something out of a nightmare—metal trees, whirring fountains, and a house that ticked like a giant clock. Instead, Clara led me through a garden so pristine it could have been painted. The hedges were perfectly trimmed, the flowers vibrant even in the dimming light, and the gravel path crunched pleasantly underfoot.

The house loomed ahead, a towering mansion that seemed pulled straight from a Victorian novel. Its stone façade was elegant, with tall windows that gleamed faintly in the light of the gas lamps lining the garden.

Clara ushered me inside, her brisk footsteps echoing against the polished marble floors. The interior was just as grand as the exterior, where sweeping staircases, gilded mirrors, and chandeliers cast a warm glow over everything. It was beautiful, yes, but it also felt strange. Like I was walking through a museum where everything was too perfect, too still.

"This way," Clara said, leading me up the stairs and down a long hallway. She opened a door at the end, revealing a guest room larger than my entire apartment back home.

The bed alone was enough to make me pause— an enormous thing with carved wooden posts and a canopy that looked like it belonged in a palace. A wardrobe stood against one wall, its doors open to reveal rows of fine dresses, and a small vanity table held an array of brushes and bottles.

"Wait here," Clara said, setting the bundle of clothes she'd brought on the bed. "I'll help you dress."

I frowned. "Help me dress? I can manage, thanks."

She snorted. "No, you can't."

I looked at the gown she had unfolded on the bed

next to me. A deep green silk dress with layers of lace and a neckline that screamed you're going to need help breathing.

"Oh no," I said, backing away. "I'm not wearing that."

"Yes, you are," Clara said, hands on her hips. "You're a guest here, and you'll dress like one."

What followed was a battle of wills—and a corset. Clara won, of course, though not without a fair amount of muttering on both sides. The corset was every bit as uncomfortable as I'd imagined, and by the time I was laced into the gown, I felt like a sausage stuffed into a very expensive casing.

"Why anyone thought this was a good idea," I grumbled, tugging at the neckline, "is beyond me."

Clara stepped back, surveying her work with a critical eye. "There. You look like a proper lady now."

"I feel like a trussed turkey."

She smirked. "A very fine turkey."

I sighed, sitting carefully on the edge of the bed. "Do I really have to wear this? Can't I have something more practical?"

Clara raised an eyebrow. "Practical? You're a lady."

"I'm not a lady," I said firmly. "I'm... well, I'm me. And I'd like to be able to breathe, thanks."

Clara rolled her eyes but nodded. "You should accept that you're a guest in a proper household now. You'll need to act accordingly."

As she turned to leave, her gaze lingered on the pendant around my neck. "That clock," she said thoughtfully. "It's out of time."

I froze. "What?"

She nodded toward it. "The hands aren't moving. You should ask the master to fix it. He'll know what to do."

Before I could respond, she swept out of the room, leaving me alone with my thoughts.

Dinner proved to be another ordeal.

The dining room was as grand as the rest of the house, with a long table set for two and enough silverware to arm a small army. Clara hovered near the door, whispering instructions as I navigated the unfamiliar terrain of Victorian etiquette.

"Start from the outside and work your way in," she hissed as I stared at the array of cutlery.

I nodded, mimicking Clara's instructions as best I could, though the array of silverware still felt like a minefield. My stomach rumbled, a mundane counterpoint to the nervous flutter in my chest. When Thaddeus entered, his usual calm precision somehow amplified the sudden rush of warmth I felt. It wasn't just relief at seeing him again—it was something more complex, a budding affection mixed with a lingering unease.

"You look... well," he said, his tone carefully neutral.

"I feel like I'm in a costume," I admitted, earning a faint smile from him.

His gaze lingered on the pendant. "The clock," he said, his voice soft. "How long have you had it?"

Before I could respond, the pendant began to hum.

It wasn't loud—more like a faint vibration against my chest—but it was enough to make me freeze. A moment later, the humming grew louder, and I realized it wasn't just sound—it was heat. The pendant was warming against my skin, the metal growing hotter by the second.

"Thaddeus?" I said, my voice tight with panic.

His head snapped up, his gaze locking on the pendant. "Take it off. Now."

I fumbled with the chain, my fingers trembling as the heat intensified. "I-I can't—"

Before I could finish, the pendant flashed. A burst of light erupted from it, filling the room with a strange, golden glow. For a moment, everything seemed to stop. The light pulsed once, twice, and then faded, leaving the room in silence.

I sat frozen, clutching the now-cool pendant as Thaddeus rose from his seat, his expression dark.

"What was that?" I whispered, my voice trembling.

The pendant, still radiating a faint warmth, felt alien against my skin. I fumbled with the clasp, my fingers shaking too badly to unfasten it. Finally, I managed to slide it off my neck and set it on the table, my gaze fixed on it as if it might explode again.

Thaddeus didn't answer right away. Instead, he reached across the table, his hand brushing against the pendant. "It's reacting," he said quietly. "To you."

I stared at him, my heart pounding. "Reacting to me? What does that even mean?"

My chest tightened as the words sank in. The pendant wasn't just a strange artifact—it was tied to me somehow. Whatever this thing was, whatever it meant, I was part of it now. And that terrified me more than the heat or the light ever could.

"It means…" he said, his voice grim, "… we don't have as much time as I thought to work out how the pendant works or to get you back safely to your time."

CHAPTER 8

*E*velyn

The golden light from the pendant still shimmered faintly, lingering in the room's corners like the ghost of a dying star. For a few breathless seconds, it felt as if the entire world had stopped—the clocks' ticking muffled, the fire's crackle distant.

My heart pounded in my chest, each beat a frantic echo of the pendant's pulse. It should have been still, inert like any ordinary piece of glass. But even though it no longer glowed, I could feel it—an almost imperceptible vibration in the air, like the room was holding its breath.

"What... what just happened?" I asked, my voice

trembling. My hands hovered above the pendant, reluctant to touch it again. It lay innocently on the table, its surface gleaming faintly in the firelight, but it felt wrong—alive in a way I couldn't explain.

Thaddeus didn't answer immediately. He now kneeled beside me at the table, his mechanical hand outstretched, hovering just above the pendant's surface. His fingers twitched slightly as if the thought of touching it unsettled even him. For the first time since I'd met him, his calm, collected demeanor cracked ever so slightly.

"The pendant reacts to disturbances in the temporal field, yes, but this is something else. It's as if it's recognizing you, Evelyn. Whatever brought you here, it's tied to more than just the pendant."

"To me," I whispered. The realization settled over me like a lead weight. "It lit up when I first touched it, but it hasn't done anything like this before. Why?"

Thaddeus exhaled sharply and pushed himself to his feet, beginning to pace the room. "It shouldn't have reacted at all," he muttered, more to himself than to me.

His metal arm clicked faintly as he flexed his fingers, his movements sharp and agitated. "The pendant is supposed to be inert. Its energy activates only in the presence of temporal anomalies or..." He stopped mid-stride, turning to face me. His expression was unreadable, but his eyes burned with intensity. "Or to someone of the bloodline of the creator."

I blinked at him, the words barely registering. "My ancestor made this?" I echoed, shaking my head.

"Evelyn." His tone was calm but firm, cutting through my panic. "I know this is overwhelming. But right now, we need to focus." He gestured toward the pendant, still lying on the table between us. "The fact that it reacted to you is significant. The pendant doesn't just light up for no reason. Now it is activated by your touch, it has become a tool, a sensor for disturbances in the temporal field. Whatever it sensed, whatever caused this..." He gestured again, his expression darkening. "It had recharged and let off the excess energy, I suppose."

"What?" My voice rose.

"The pendant is reacting to something in your presence, amplified now that you survived time travel, but it's clever. It's changing."

"Changing? What do you mean?"

"Look at it," he said, nodding toward the pendant.

I hesitated, then stood and leaned closer. The glass surface gleamed faintly in the firelight, and as I studied it, I noticed something I hadn't seen before—faint etchings, delicate and intricate, spiraling across the glass like frost on a windowpane. They seemed to shift as I watched, the patterns morphing ever so slightly as if alive.

"These markings weren't here before," Thaddeus said, his voice tight. He reached out, his metal fingers brushing lightly against the glass. "It's evolving. Responding to your activation and becoming something more powerful and chaotic."

I took a step back, a shiver running down my spine. "That sounds… dangerous."

"It could be," he admitted grimly. "If it continues to react like this, it could destabilize completely. And if that happens…" he trailed off, his jaw tightening.

"What happens if it destabilizes?" I pressed, my voice barely above a whisper.

"I saw it happen once," Thaddeus said, his voice low. "A rift opened in a small town, barely more than a village. One moment, it was there, full of people, their lives, their memories. The next, it was gone—not destroyed but erased as if it had never existed. And the worst part?" He paused, his jaw tightening. "No one remembered it. Not even me, until I found the records. That's what a rift can do, Evelyn. It doesn't just destroy, it rewrites."

I swallowed hard, the air in the room suddenly feeling too thin. "But… I didn't cause this, right? It's the pendant, not me."

Thaddeus hesitated, his jaw tightening ever so

slightly. "The pendant shouldn't be doing this," he admitted. "It's unstable, yes, but not like this. Whatever's happening, it's tied to you, and the longer it reacts, the closer we get to a rift. If that happens…" he trailed off, his voice dropping.

"What?" I pressed, my voice a whisper. "What happens if it reacts too much?"

His hand brushed against the pendant as if testing its weight. "You won't just lose your way back home, Evelyn. You'll lose your life."

A rift. The word sent a chill through me, though I didn't fully understand what it meant. "So, what do we do?" I asked.

"We need to get the Chronarium back," he said simply. "It could be the only thing that can stabilize the pendant's energy and possibly give us answers about why this is happening. Without it…" he shook his head, his expression grim, "… we don't have much time."

Before I could respond, a sharp knock echoed through the room. The sound startled us both, snapping the tension taut like a wire. I turned toward the door as Clara appeared in the doorway, her face pale.

"Mr. Blackwood," she said, her voice hushed. "This just arrived."

She held out a folded envelope, sealed with an

elaborate crest in dark red wax. Her hands trembled slightly as she passed it to Thaddeus. "There was no messenger. It was just left on the doorstep."

Thaddeus's brow furrowed as he took the envelope, turning it over in his hands. His gaze lingered on the wax seal for a moment before he broke it open. His eyes quickly scanned the contents, his expression hardening with each line. When he finally looked up, his face was unreadable, but his voice was tight.

"It seems..." he said, "... we've been summoned."

Clara stepped forward, her tone low. "Lord Abernathy. He's famous for this sort of thing. A collector of rare artifacts, a patron of science, and a man who loves control. If he's sent this, it's because he knows something we don't."

"Abernathy doesn't just collect artifacts," Thaddeus said, his voice low and measured. "He collects people. His soirées are where alliances are forged and destroyed. If he sees you as a threat, he won't hesitate to neutralize you. Politely, of course. With champagne in hand."

A chill ran down my spine. "Neutralize me? What does that mean?"

Clara exchanged a glance with Thaddeus. "It means..." she said slowly, "... that Abernathy is as dangerous as he is charming."

I frowned. "Abernathy? The Abernathy you mentioned earlier? The one who financed your experiments?"

Thaddeus muttered under his breath, "Abernathy never does anything without an angle. He doesn't send invitations… he sets traps."

My stomach twisted. "You think he knows about me? About the pendant?"

"He's obsessed with time. Control isn't just a game to him, it's an addiction. If he knows what the pendant can do, he won't stop until it's his. And if he's sent this invitation, it's because he already knows more than we do," Thaddeus said, his voice sharp.

I swallowed hard, a fresh wave of unease washing over me. "So, what do we do?"

Thaddeus folded the letter and tucked it into his coat. His expression was grim but resolute.

"We go. Abernathy may be the only way to find the Chronarium."

"And if it isn't?" I asked hesitantly.

"Then someone at his soirée knows where it is."

I sighed, running a hand through my hair. I didn't want to go. I didn't want to charm some manipulative aristocrat who probably already knew more about me than I did. But what choice did I have? If this Abernathy had the answers, I couldn't walk away. Not now.

"Fine," I muttered.

Clara gave me a once-over, her lips twitching into a faint smile. "You'll need a proper gown," she said. "Abernathy's parties are strictly high society. No one will take you seriously looking like that. You will need to earn his trust."

I stared at Clara, incredulous. "I don't even know the man. And what makes you think I'm the kind of person Abernathy would trust?"

Thaddeus's expression didn't waver. "Because you're new. You're unknown."

Clara smirked, folding her arms. "Don't worry. Abernathy's insufferable, but he's predictable. Just let him think he's the smartest man in the room. He'll eat it up."

"I'm not exactly known for my charm," I muttered, my voice tight with nerves.

"Just be yourself," Thaddeus said, already halfway to his workshop. "That would win him over." He stood and moved over to me. "We leave tonight."

He picked up the pendant, the lack of glow unsettling. "For now, this is the best place to keep it." His fingers, metal and flesh, grazed my skin as he fastened the chain, the touch sending a jolt of unease through me, mixed with desire.

"What if it reacts again?" I asked, my voice laced with apprehension.

"Then we'll deal with it," he said, his tone brisk. "But for now, it's your only connection to your time. And possibly your only way out of this one."

I swallowed, the pendant's weight a cold reminder of the danger we were facing. How could I possibly navigate Abernathy's world with this unpredictable artifact burning against my skin?

CHAPTER 9

*T*haddeus

The carriage gently swayed as it rolled over the cobblestone streets, the sound of the wheels a faint clatter against the quiet night. I sat opposite Evelyn, my hands clasped in my lap, the faint hum of the pendant's energy still echoing in my mind. I had hoped the artifact would settle after its earlier outburst, but instead, it seemed to pulse faintly as if aware of the looming danger ahead. Danger in the form of Abernathy.

I had taken every precaution I could without drawing unnecessary attention. Bastion, my trusted manservant, rode on top with the driver, his sharp eyes scanning the streets for anything—or anyone—out of place. Harris, who had once chased down thieves with a speed and determination that still impressed me, was armed tonight, though discreetly. His presence brought me some measure of reassurance, though it wasn't enough to ease the knot of unease in my chest.

Inside the carriage, Clara sat beside Evelyn, her presence as a chaperone lending an air of propriety to our outing. It was a necessary measure, one I had insisted on to avoid raising eyebrows and questions. Clara, ever the social butterfly, had embraced the role with enthusiasm, her cheerful chatter filling the otherwise tense silence.

I glanced at Evelyn. She was staring out the window, her chin resting on her hand, her expression distant. She had changed into a gown Clara had miraculously procured—a deep green that shimmered in the low light, with intricate embroidery along the bodice. It suited her, though I doubted she felt comfortable in it. Evelyn didn't seem the type to enjoy corsets and frills. And yet, despite everything—the corset, the gown, the unfathomable leap through time—she seemed to be handling it all with a calm I couldn't quite comprehend.

"Are you nervous?" Clara asked from beside her, the excitement in her voice barely restrained.

Evelyn turned from the window and gave a half smile. "Terrified, actually. But I'm trying to pretend I'm not."

Clara grinned. "You're doing a marvelous job."

I allowed myself a small, fleeting smile at Evelyn's response. She had a strength I admired, though I doubted she realized it herself. My mind, however, quickly returned to the task at hand. Abernathy had to be stopped, and every instinct told me tonight would be pivotal.

The carriage slowed, the clatter of the wheels softening as we neared our destination. Harris's voice drifted down through the small opening near the driver's seat. "All clear, sir."

I straightened and adjusted my cuffs. "Stay close to me," I said, my tone calm but firm as I looked at Evelyn. "Clara, keep an eye on her."

Clara rolled her eyes but smiled. "I think I can manage that."

"I've been meaning to ask," I said, turning back to Evelyn. "The future... your time. What's it like?"

Evelyn blinked at me, caught off guard, and sat up a little straighter. "What's it like? Well, it's..." She hesitated, then let out a soft laugh. "Loud. Busy. Fast. There's so much happening constantly, it's hard to keep up."

"Faster than steam engines or telegraphs?" I asked, genuinely curious.

"Oh, much faster," she said with a small smile. "We have cars, machines that can travel faster than any horse, and planes, which can fly through the air and cross oceans in hours. And then there's the internet, which... well, it's like a web connecting everyone and everything. You can send messages instantly, watch moving pictures, learn anything you want, all from a little device in your hand."

I stared at her, unable to hide my astonishment. "Moving pictures? Messages through the air? It sounds... impossible."

"It probably does," Evelyn admitted. "But it's normal where I'm from. Honestly, we don't even think about how strange it is. It's just life. But we don't have automatons like... you."

"Fascinating." I leaned back, my mind racing. For all my tinkering and inventing, for all the brilliance I prided myself on, I could barely fathom the world she described.

Was it truly possible to advance so far? To transcend the limits of steam and metal, of wires and gears? More than that, though, I felt a pang of something I couldn't quite name. Longing, perhaps, maybe envy. She had traveled through time and done what I had spent my life dreaming of, and she spoke of it as though it was a burden.

"What about you?" I asked quietly. "Do you miss it? Your time?"

Evelyn hesitated, her gaze dropping to her hands. "I don't know," she said finally. "I thought I would, but... there's not much to miss. My parents are gone. I don't have siblings. I had a job and a tiny apartment. That's about it."

I frowned. "No one is looking for you? No one will notice you're gone?"

"No one will notice I'm gone," she said softly, her voice steady but hollow. "It's strange, isn't it? You think your life means something, that you leave a mark. But now that I'm here, I realize it doesn't. My time will go on without me, and no one will know I'm missing." She looked down at her hands, her fingers twisting in her lap. "Maybe that's why this doesn't feel as terrifying as it should. There's nothing to go back to."

Her voice was calm, but there was sadness beneath it that I couldn't ignore. I wanted to say something, but the words wouldn't come.

"Come to think of it..." she continued, "... I could well be the last of my bloodline. My father's brother died without having children, and my mom was an only child. Could this have something to do with the pendant reacting to me? As if it knows I'm the last chance it has to activate?"

"It could well be," I agreed. "This makes it even more important we find out how it works." I straightened, my thoughts shifting to the task ahead. "We're here," I said, glancing out the window.

I had worked my entire life to unravel the mysteries of time, chase it, and control it. Yet here was this woman, plucked from the future and dropped into a world that must seem barbaric and alien to her, and she was adapting with remarkable ease.

The mansion loomed before us, its grand façade aglow with golden light. Guests in elegant attire moved up the wide staircase, disappearing into the glittering hall beyond. Music drifted through the open doors—violins and a piano, refined and haunting. The carriage came to a stop, and I stepped out first, offering a hand to Clara and then to Evelyn. She accepted it, her grip firm, and I was struck again by how out of place she must feel. Yet she held her head high, her expression determined.

"You're sure about this?" I asked her quietly.

"No," she said. "But let's do it anyway."

I allowed myself the faintest smile. "Good answer."

We ascended the steps together, Clara chattering excitedly about the grandeur of the event while Evelyn remained silent. I scanned the crowd as we entered, my gaze searching for Abernathy. I spotted him near the far end of the room, surrounded by a small group of admirers. He turned as if sensing our arrival, his sharp eyes landing on Evelyn almost immediately. A slow smile spread across his face, and my stomach sank.

I leaned closer to Evelyn, my voice low. "He's already seen us."

I knew Abernathy well enough to recognize the danger behind his smile. He wasn't just a rival, he was a predator, and if he suspected Evelyn was more than she appeared, he wouldn't hesitate to use her to his advantage. Abernathy didn't play fair, and he didn't forgive mistakes.

Evelyn stiffened, her eyes locking with Abernathy's across the room. "Good," she said softly, but a tremor in her voice betrayed her nerves.

I hesitated for a moment before offering my hand. "Dance with me."

Evelyn blinked, her brow furrowing. "What?"

"Dance," I repeated, my voice steady but urgent. "We need to blend in. Besides..." My gaze flicked back to Abernathy. "If he's going to watch us, let's give him something to look at."

Her lips parted in surprise, but she took my hand. My grip was firm and grounding, allowing me to lead her onto the dance floor. The music swelled around us, a waltz that was both elegant and haunting.

I placed my hand on her waist, guiding her in smooth, purposeful movements. The music swirled around us, a haunting waltz that seemed to echo in Evelyn's chest. She could feel the heat of my hand through the fabric of her gown, my grip steady and grounding. The press of the crowd around us faded into a blur of color and motion, leaving only the two of us in sharp focus. Evelyn followed my lead, her steps hesitant at first but growing more confident as we moved together.

"You're a natural," Evelyn murmured, her voice soft against my ear.

"Years of tedious practice," I replied, forcing a lightness I didn't feel. "Diplomats and their obligatory waltzes." All I could think about was the way she fit against me, the subtle scent of her perfume, the warmth radiating from her skin.

"And this?" she asked, her gaze meeting mine. "Is this another political maneuver?"

"No," I whispered, my voice thick with something I couldn't name. This wasn't a dance, but a connection, a spark igniting in the space between us. My internal mechanisms hummed, a low, steady thrum that echoed the sudden, overwhelming desire that coursed through me.

My hand tightened on hers, my fingers tracing the delicate curve of her wrist. "Evelyn..."

She shivered as my breath brushed against her ear.

The music faded, leaving a silence that felt both intimate and dangerous. We stood frozen, our breaths mingling in the still air, the world around us a blurry backdrop to the intensity of the moment.

For a heartbeat, we didn't move. My hand lingered on her waist, and Evelyn leaned toward me. My eyes flicked to her lips, my face impossibly close to hers.

"Enjoying yourselves?" Abernathy's voice cut through the air like a knife, smooth and mocking.

We broke apart instantly, Evelyn stepping back as if she'd been burned. I turned to face Abernathy, my expression hardening.

Abernathy approached with the smooth confidence of a predator. The crowd seemed to shift subtly as he passed, their conversations quieting as his presence drew their attention. His dark hair gleamed under the chandeliers, every movement measured and calculated. I noticed his sharp eyes scanned the room, missing nothing, his smile polite but cold.

"Thaddeus," he said, his tone dripping with false warmth. "It's been too long."

"Not long enough," I replied evenly.

"I miss funding your inventions. Yours always had more success."

"Well, I have other means now."

He turned his gaze to Evelyn. "And who is this?"

"This is Miss Evelyn…" I hesitated, realizing too late that we hadn't discussed a cover story.

"Williams," Evelyn said smoothly, extending a hand. "A pleasure to meet you, Mr. Abernathy."

Abernathy took her hand, his smile widening. "The pleasure is mine." He glanced at me. "You've brought a charming companion. How uncharacteristic."

I clenched my jaw but said nothing.

"Miss Williams…" Abernathy said, releasing her hand, "… would you honor me with a dance?"

I stiffened. Evelyn glanced at me briefly before smiling at Abernathy. "Of course."

Abernathy offered his arm, and Evelyn took it, allowing him to lead her toward the dance floor. I watched them go, my hands curling into fists at my sides. Clara touched my arm. "She'll be fine," she murmured.

I didn't answer. Across the room, Abernathy leaned in to speak to Evelyn, his smile sharp and predatory. I could only hope she was as composed as she seemed.

CHAPTER 10

$\mathcal{E}$velyn

The ballroom glittered like something out of a dream—or maybe a nightmare. Chandeliers dripped with crystals that scattered the light, casting shifting patterns across the polished floor. Women in extravagant dresses floated past, their laughter rising above the hum of the string quartet. The scent of beeswax candles and expensive perfume hung heavily in the air.

And here I was, in the middle of it all, feeling like an awkward imposter in borrowed silk.

Abernathy led me onto the dance floor with the easy confidence of someone who knew they belonged. His grip was firm but not unpleasant, and his smile never wavered. I tried not to look back at Thaddeus, though I could feel his gaze burning into my back.

"You're quite the mystery, Miss Williams," Abernathy said, his voice smooth as honey. "I don't believe I've had the pleasure of seeing you at one of my gatherings before. Where are you from?"

I forced a smile, hoping it didn't look as fake as it felt. "A small town," I said vaguely. "Far from here."

Abernathy chuckled, his eyes never leaving mine. "How intriguing. And what brings you to our little corner of the world?"

The music swelled, and he spun me in a graceful turn. My pulse quickened, but I kept my voice steady. "Curiosity, mostly. I've heard so much about your collection, Mr. Abernathy. I couldn't resist seeing it for myself."

His smile widened, but his expression was sharp, like a blade hidden beneath silk. "My collection, you say? I wasn't aware it had garnered such a reputation."

"Oh, it has," I said lightly. "Artifacts, curiosities... I imagine there's no one else who could rival your expertise."

His eyes glittered, and I knew I had said the right thing. People like Abernathy thrived on flattery, and

I was more than willing to play along if it meant keeping him off-balance.

"You flatter me, Miss Williams," he said, his voice dropping to a conspiratorial murmur. "But tell me, how is it you know so much about my work? I don't recall seeing your name in any of my circles."

My heart skipped a beat, but I kept my smile in place. "Oh, I'm not part of any circle," I said with a small laugh. "I just... pay attention to the right whispers."

Abernathy's grip on my waist tightened ever so slightly, but his expression remained smooth. "Whispers are dangerous things. They have a way of leading people into trouble."

The warning in his tone wasn't subtle, but I refused to let him intimidate me. "Sometimes trouble is worth the risk," I said, meeting his gaze head-on.

For a moment, his smile faltered. Then it returned, sharper than ever. "I do like a woman with spirit," he said. "It's such a rare quality these days."

The music shifted into a slower, more deliberate rhythm, and Abernathy pulled me closer. I could feel the heat of his hand through the fabric of my dress, and I resisted the urge to pull away.

Abernathy smiled again, but this time, there was no mistaking the calculation in his eyes. He was enjoying this game, but he also wasn't fooled. He knew I wasn't just some random guest, and he was going to figure out why I was there.

The pendant beneath my dress felt heavier than ever, its faint hum vibrating against my skin. I could only pray he didn't sense it, though the way his eyes flicked toward my chest sent a shiver of unease through me.

The music shifted again, signaling the end of the dance. "I do hope you'll allow me to show you my collection later. I suspect you'll find it... enlightening."

"I'd be delighted," I said, though the idea of being alone with him in a room full of ancient, possibly cursed artifacts was about as appealing as jumping into a snake pit.

Abernathy released me with a bow, and I curtsied in return, my heart pounding so hard I was sure he could hear it. As he turned away, heading toward another group of guests, I allowed myself a moment to breathe.

I scanned the room for Thaddeus and found him standing near the edge of the dance floor, his sharp features tense as he watched me. Clara was beside him, chatting animatedly with someone, though her eyes darted toward me every few seconds.

I crossed the room quickly, weaving through the

crowd until I was close enough for Thaddeus to speak without raising my voice.

"Well?" he asked, his tone clipped.

"He's suspicious," I said quietly. "But I think I held my own."

Thaddeus's jaw tightened. "What did he say?"

"He asked questions. Where I'm from, why I'm here... nothing too pointed, but he's definitely fishing for something." I hesitated, glancing toward the far end of the room where Abernathy was now laughing with a group of elegantly dressed men and women. "He wants to show me his collection."

Thaddeus frowned. "That could be dangerous. I'm certain he knows you've time-traveled."

"I know," I said, trying to keep my voice steady. "But it might be our best chance to find what we're looking for."

Clara appeared at my side, her expression bright but her voice low. "Whatever you said, it worked. He's watching you like a hawk."

I resisted the urge to look back at Abernathy. "Let him watch. As long as he doesn't figure out what I'm really doing, we're fine."

Thaddeus didn't look convinced. His eyes searched mine, his expression unreadable, and for a moment, the noise of the ballroom seemed to fade.

"You were brave out there," he said finally, his voice softer than I expected.

I felt a flush of warmth at the compliment, but I brushed it aside. "Brave or stupid. Let's hope it doesn't come back to bite us."

The pendant thrummed faintly against my skin again, and I touched it absently, my fingers brushing over the fabric of my dress. It had brought me there, and I would do anything to find out why.

"Miss Williams, would you like another dance?" Abernathy approached me again. It was the last thing I wanted to do. I'd barely caught my breath from dancing.

"Of course." I held out my gloved hand and allowed him to direct me to the dance floor.

CHAPTER 11

$\mathcal{T}$haddeus

The ballroom shimmered with the artifice of civility —gilded chandeliers, polished floors, and a sea of men and women in silks and finery, all pretending they weren't watching one another like hawks. I adjusted my cravat for the fifth time that evening and allowed myself a sip of champagne, though it did little to soothe my nerves. My eyes darted constantly to Evelyn, who was now gliding across the floor in Abernathy's arms. I hated every second of it.

Evelyn looked poised as ever, her brilliant green gown setting her apart from the sea of neutral-toned dresses. But I could see the tension in her shoulders, the way her smile faltered when Abernathy leaned in too close. She was holding her own, but that didn't make it any easier to watch.

"They make a striking pair, don't they?" I glanced to my left to see Clara looking nervous. She'd been stationed near the refreshments table, blending seamlessly into the background as servants were meant to, though her sharp eyes missed nothing.

"I wouldn't call it striking," I muttered, my jaw tight.

"Oh, don't pout," Clara said, smirking. "She's doing exactly what she's supposed to. Look at him. He's eating out of her hand."

I didn't respond. Abernathy wasn't eating out of anyone's hand. He was a predator, and Evelyn was the prey. I wanted to storm across the room, tear her away from him, and throw the man out onto the street where he belonged.

But I didn't.

Because Evelyn had insisted she could handle herself. And because I knew she was right. If we wanted any hope of discovering what Abernathy knew about the rift and the Chronarium, this was the only way.

Still, I couldn't stop the wave of relief that washed over me when the dance ended, and Abernathy led her back toward the edge of the ballroom, bowing over her hand before leaving her with a smile that made my skin crawl.

"She's fine," Clara said, nudging me. "Stop hovering and talk to her." I didn't need further encouragement.

I crossed the room to where Evelyn stood, her hands clasped tightly in front of her.

"Thaddeus, how are you? Terrible business with the thief today." I turned to see Charles, another inventor, approaching me. I couldn't stop and talk.

I turned to keep moving toward Evelyn, but she was gone.

I didn't like this one bit. I had to assume Abernathy was showing her his collection, but that only made my clogs spin heatedly.

I spent the next half hour doing what I could to distract myself. I spoke with two inventors who were debating the merits of steam propulsion over electric motors, though I barely registered their words. I nodded politely as Professor James Hyatt from Oxford attempted to explain his theory on temporal elasticity, but my thoughts remained on Evelyn. And why they were gone for so long.

I glanced around the room, searching for them, but neither was anywhere to be seen. My chest tightened. "Excuse me," I said abruptly, cutting off a particularly long-winded explanation from Hyatt and turning toward the nearest door to get outside.

The cool night air hit me like a slap as I stepped outside. The garden was quiet, the soft glow of lanterns illuminating the neatly trimmed hedges and stone pathways. I scanned the grounds, my heart pounding. And then I heard it.

A scream—sharp, high-pitched, and unmistakably female. I didn't think. I ran.

The sound had come from the far side of the garden, near the servants' entrance. I rounded the corner just in time to see a man shove Evelyn into the back of a covered cart, her wrists bound and her face pale with terror.

"Evelyn!" I shouted, drawing my revolver.

The man froze for a split second before scrambling into the driver's seat. The horse whinnied, and the cart lurched forward.

I fired a shot into the air, but it did little to slow them. The cart careened down the alley, disappearing into the shadows before I could reach it.

I stopped, my hand trembling around the revolver. Evelyn was gone.

CHAPTER 12

$\mathcal{E}$velyn

The cart hit a deep rut in the road, and I slammed against the wooden floorboards. My head pulsed where it had struck the edge earlier, and the ache in my shoulders had settled into a dull, relentless burn.

My wrists were bound tightly in front of me with a rough rope, and every time I shifted, the fibers scraped against my skin, leaving it raw. The skin beneath the rope felt hot and swollen, and I could feel the sticky warmth of blood where the fibers had cut deep.

I tried not to move, but the cart rocked again, nearly pitching me sideways, and I braced myself against the wall to keep from being thrown. I was so tired, my body screaming for rest, but I couldn't give in. Not now.

Above me, Abernathy's voice carried over the rumble of the wheels. "Faster!" he barked, sharp and impatient. "We can't afford any delays."

My stomach twisted, not just from the nauseating motion of the cart but from the cold knot of fear tightening in my chest. Abernathy had taken me. My mind raced, replaying the moment his men had grabbed me, the glint of satisfaction in his eyes as they dragged me away. And now I was here, trapped, heading toward—what?

Could I even get out of this alive? My mind screamed at me to try, to fight, but a nagging voice whispered that it was hopeless. Abernathy was too clever, too prepared. And Thaddeus, could he even find me?

The pendant around my neck swayed with the cart's motion, its faint hum the only constant in the chaos. Its energy was steady, almost soothing, but I couldn't rely on it to get me out of this timeline to safety. I didn't even understand it. Not completely.

The cart slowed, the wheels crunching over gravel before coming to a stop. I heard Abernathy jump down, his boots hitting the ground with a definite thud. "Get her inside," he ordered, his voice calm and clipped.

Moments later, the tarp above me was yanked back, and two men loomed over me. Their faces were hard and impassive, and they didn't bother with words as they climbed into the cart and grabbed me. One of them wrapped his hands around my arms, hauling me upright, while the other grabbed my legs.

"Let me go!" I shouted, twisting against their grip. My voice was raw, cracked from the dry air and my panic, but I didn't stop. I kicked, writhing as hard as I could, but they didn't even flinch.

Abernathy appeared in front of me, his silhouette sharp against the faint glow of the building ahead. He tilted his head, watching my struggles with quiet amusement.

"Miss Williams," he said, shaking his head. "You really should save your energy. You'll need it."

His calmness only fueled my rage. I wanted to scream at him, to wipe that smug look off his face, but my words would mean nothing to him. The fury burned in my chest, hot and steady. I wouldn't let him win.

The men carried me, their hands unrelenting. I forced myself to go limp, letting my body sag between them.

"The boss says we'll need the machine running by midnight," one of the men muttered.

"If we can get the Chronarium to stabilize—"

The other man cut him off with a sharp glance in my direction. "Shut up. She doesn't need to hear that."

I kept my eyes half-closed, breathing shallow, pretending not to notice. But I filed the word away, Chronarium. Abernathy was behind the theft.

They carried me toward a building that loomed out of the darkness like something from a nightmare —a massive, crumbling structure with sharp, uneven angles. Gas lights flickered from windows, their pale glow casting long, jagged shadows across the gravel. The air reeked of oil and rust, and the closer we got, the harder it became to breathe.

The men carried me through what appeared to be a servants' staircase, rickety and unkept, dark and dingy, farther into this monster's home.

The heavy iron door creaked as it swung open, and the men carried me inside. The room swallowed me whole, its vastness disorienting. Machines lined the walls, their hulking shapes barely visible in the dim light. Wires snaked across the floor, criss-crossing like a web, and the hum of electricity vibrated in the air, low and constant.

I craned my neck, trying to take in as much as I

could. The machines were massive and strange, with glowing tubes and flickering dials. I didn't recognize any of them, but I could feel their faint and unsettling energy brushing against my skin like static.

If Abernathy got what he wanted, if he unlocked the pendant's secrets, what would it mean for Thaddeus? For me? For everyone? That thought terrified me more than the machines or the ropes biting into my wrists. I had to get out of here, no matter what.

In the center of the room was a long metal table, its surface gleaming under the harsh light of an overhead lamp. My stomach twisted at the sight of it, and I thrashed harder against the men's grip.

"No," I said, my voice breaking. "No, you can't—"

They ignored me. They dumped me onto the table, the cold metal biting into my skin through the thin fabric of my dress. Before I could move, they cut the ropes binding my hands and strapped my wrists and ankles with thick leather restraints.

I struggled, pulling against the straps, but they didn't budge. The leather was too strong and too tight.

Abernathy stepped into view, his expression calm but his eyes alight with something sharp and cruel. "You really should relax," he said, his voice almost gentle. "This will be much easier if you cooperate."

He leaned closer, his gaze fixed on the pendant

around my neck. His smile widened, slow and resigned as if he'd just uncovered a great secret.

"Fascinating," he murmured, reaching out to touch it.

"Don't," I snapped, jerking away from him as best I could.

His hand paused, hovering just above the pendant as its light intensified. Then he straightened, clasping his hands behind his back as he paced. "Now..." he said, his tone almost conversational, "... let's talk. What do you know about the pendant? And more importantly, how does it work?"

I didn't answer. I couldn't. Besides, I didn't know.

Abernathy stopped, turning to look at me. "Silence won't save you, Miss Williams." His voice was soft, but there was steel beneath it. "You'll tell me what I want to know. Eventually."

He leaned closer, his smile returning. "Everyone breaks, you see. You'll tell me everything, sooner or later."

He stepped back, gesturing to the men who had brought me in. "Watch her," he said. "I'll be back shortly."

The moment he was gone, I tested the restraints again. My wrists were raw from the ropes earlier, and now the leather straps cut into the same tender skin. My arms ached, and a sharp pain shot through my head, but I couldn't stop.

I scanned the room, forcing myself to focus. The machines hummed faintly, their dials flickering. Wires crisscrossed the floor, and near the far wall, I spotted a door. It was slightly ajar, the darkness beyond it calling to me.

The strap around my left wrist had loosened— just barely. I twisted my hand, ignoring the pain as the leather scraped against my skin. Slowly, agonizingly, I managed to slip free.

I worked on the other straps, my hands trembling. Finally, I was free.

As I slid off the table, my hand brushed against a small metal object on the floor—a bolt or a piece of machinery. I grabbed it instinctively, curling my fingers around it. It wasn't much, but it was better than nothing, and I slipped through the open door.

The hallway beyond was dim, the shadows deep and unsettling. Pipes lined the walls, their surfaces slick with condensation. I moved as quietly as I could, my feet barely making a sound against the floor.

I spotted a faint glow at the end of the hallway. My chest tightened with hope, and I quickened my pace, ignoring the pain in my legs. Freedom was so close. I could almost taste it.

A shout echoed behind me, sharp and angry. My breath caught, and I broke into a run. My muscles screamed in protest, but I forced myself to keep moving.

I turned a corner away from the faint glow, trying to lose those chasing me. The hallways twisted and turned in every direction. The air grew colder, and the smell of oil grew stronger.

Before I could take another step, strong hands grabbed my arms, yanking me backward. I twisted, kicking and thrashing, but it was no use.

Abernathy's voice rang out, cold and triumphant. "Did you really think you could escape, Miss Williams?"

The guards dragged me back to the lab, their grip unrelenting, taking the machine I had stolen from my hands. They tied me back to the table, pulling the straps even tighter this time. Abernathy leaned over me, his smile sharp and cruel.

"You'll find…" he said softly, "… I'm not so easily outwitted."

I shuddered, knowing that I would lose to him if I didn't manage to overcome the odds against me.

CHAPTER 13

*T*haddeus

The workshop was too quiet. The hum of machinery, once a soothing rhythm to my frantic mind, now felt hollow and lifeless.

My tools lay scattered across the workbench, abandoned when the letter arrived. A single sheet of cream-colored paper, folded once, rested next to a barely touched cup of tea.

Abernathy's message had been brief but unmistakable. *I have her.*

My fists clenched as I paced. I had read the note hours ago, but the words still felt like a noose tightening around my throat. Evelyn was gone, and it was my fault.

This wasn't the first time someone I cared about had paid the price for my choices. I told myself I'd learned from my mistakes and that I'd never let my work endanger anyone again.

I stopped in front of the mirror over the small fireplace and stared at the wreck of a man looking back at me. My shirt was wrinkled, my cravat loosened, and my hair disheveled. I hardly recognized myself. Society's polished inventor was gone—what remained was a man unraveling.

The pendant. I could still see it in my mind, hanging around Evelyn's neck the last time I saw her. Its strange etchings had fascinated me, its significance clawed at me.

Abernathy must have known what it was. He wouldn't go through this much trouble for Evelyn unless the pendant was involved.

Somehow, it was the key to all of this—and she'd trusted me to protect her. And I'd failed. I couldn't waste any more time. I had to rescue her. There was one person who might be able to help me.

The fog pressed against me as I stormed through London's streets, my long coat trailing behind me. The city felt different tonight—more oppressive as if it sensed Evelyn's danger. Every gaslight seemed dimmer, every shadow darker.

I stopped at Inspector Grayson's house. We weren't close, but he was my best chance at finding Abernathy.

Grayson opened the door, his sharp gray eyes narrowing as he took me in.

"Thaddeus?" His voice was thick with surprise. "You look like hell."

"I don't have time for pleasantries," I snapped, brushing past him into his study. The scent of pipe smoke and leather filled the room, but I barely registered it. "I need information. Now."

Grayson followed me in, closing the door behind him. "This wouldn't have anything to do with Abernathy, would it?"

I froze. "You know something."

Grayson sighed, crossing to his sideboard and pouring himself a drink. He offered me one, but I shook my head.

"Abernathy's been under surveillance for months. Strange comings and goings at his estate. Unusual shipments. But nothing concrete enough to act on."

"What kind of shipments?" I pressed, stepping closer.

"Machines. Components. Some of it's military-grade, but most of it..." he trailed off, shaking his head. "It's like he's building something entirely new. Something we can't even begin to comprehend."

I frowned. "And no one's stopped him?"

Grayson shot me a sharp look. "You don't think I would if I could? The man's careful. Covers his tracks. And every time I get close..." He gestured vaguely, his frustration palpable. "He slips away."

"What about the theft of the Chronarium?" I demanded. "Was that him?"

Grayson paused, swirling the amber liquid in his glass before taking a sip. "Yes," he said finally. "He orchestrated it, but we aren't sure what he wants with it."

"You've been aware of this and done nothing?" My voice was dangerously low.

"We've had nothing to go on!" Grayson exploded, his control finally snapping. "Abernathy's a master manipulator, Thaddeus. He operates in the shadows, and he always wins."

I clenched my fists, the metal creaking faintly. "Not this time." The thought of Evelyn in Abernathy's clutches sent a wave of fear through me, a sensation so alien and unwelcome that it momentarily short-circuited my logic processors. "He has a woman I..." I stopped, the words failing me. *Care for.* The realization struck me with the force of a physical blow.

Grayson leaned forward, his gaze piercing. "Why does this matter so much to you? What is she to you?"

"She's..." My voice was barely a whisper, the admission a strange mix of terror and tenderness. "Evelyn's important. And if Abernathy has her, she's in danger."

Grayson's expression softened, though his tone remained brisk. "Then you're in over your head. If this woman is with Abernathy, he's not holding her for ransom. He wants something. Something she has or knows."

"The pendant," I muttered under my breath. Grayson's brows rose in question, but I didn't elaborate.

"Listen to me, Thaddeus," Grayson said, leaning forward. "Abernathy's dangerous. He's obsessed with things he doesn't understand. And he has resources you can't even begin to imagine. If you're going after him, you'll need more than your wits to get her back."

"I know how dangerous he is." My voice was low, but there was steel in it.

"All I can ask you is, is she worth it?"

"She is." My resolve was firm and unyielding.

Grayson sighed again, setting his glass down with a clink. "He's been hosting gatherings at his estate... private affairs, invitation only. There's supposed to be another one tomorrow tonight. If Evelyn's there..."

"She is," I said firmly. I didn't know how I could be so certain, but I was.

Grayson studied me for a long moment, then nodded. "I'll get you a map of the building where he's building God knows what. It's more like an estate where people can easily go missing. But Thaddeus..." He placed a hand on my shoulder, his grip firm. "Abernathy doesn't play fair."

Back at the workshop, I spread the map Grayson had given me across the workbench. My eyes scanned the layout of Abernathy's mansion. The estate was sprawling, its twisting hallways and vast rooms forming a labyrinth.

Getting in undetected would be impossible. I leaned over the map, my brow furrowed. My mind raced, calculating distances, angles, and escape routes. I'd need a distraction to draw Abernathy's attention away from Evelyn.

My gaze drifted to the sketches and formulas in my notebook. I'd been working on a prototype—a small device capable of generating a short-range electromagnetic pulse. It wasn't ready, but if I could modify it, perhaps it could disrupt Abernathy's machines. It was a gamble, but it was the best chance

I had. I set to work, my hands moving with a precision born of desperation.

Hours slipped away as I soldered wires, adjusted circuits, and tested the device. I didn't notice the sun rising until pale light crept through the workshop windows. Exhaustion tugged at my limbs, but I couldn't afford to rest.

I called for Harris and Bastion to accompany me, the two I most trusted, and we set out to rescue Evelyn.

Abernathy's estate loomed before me as I approached, its dark silhouette cutting against the morning sky. I could see carriages arriving, their occupants disappearing inside.

I stayed in the shadows with my men, slipping around to the back of the mansion.

"You stay here," I said to Harris and Bastion. "Keep watch. If I'm not back within the hour, leave."

They nodded as I slipped around the side of the house and found a small servants' entrance. I picked the lock with practiced ease. The door creaked open, and I stepped inside, my heart pounding.

The air was heavy, laced with the scent of smoke and something metallic. My footsteps were silent on the polished floors, but every creak of the wood and distant murmur of voices set my nerves on edge. I moved quickly, weaving through the building's labyrinthine halls until I reached a study.

The room was cavernous, filled with towering shelves and flickering gas lamps. It was empty, but I could hear voices nearby—Abernathy's smooth, commanding tone among them. My jaw tightened.

A sudden crash echoed from upstairs, followed by a muffled shout. My blood ran cold.

It was her.

I'd know Evelyn's voice anywhere, even strained and distant. It cut through my fear, igniting a fire in my chest. Without a second thought, I bolted for the staircase.

CHAPTER 14

$\mathcal{E}$velyn

The leather strap bit into my wrist, no matter how much I twisted against it. My palm was slick with sweat, the sharp edges of the buckles cutting into my skin, but I didn't stop pulling. If I stopped, I'd lose focus and couldn't afford that. Not when Abernathy was circling me like a predator, his footsteps echoing off the cold metal walls of the laboratory.

"Do you know what I despise most, Miss Williams?" Abernathy asked, his voice as smooth and oily as the machines humming around us. "Dishonesty." He stopped beside the table, leaning down so his face was inches from mine. "And you, my dear, are a liar."

I glared at him, refusing to flinch. "I don't know what you're talking about."

"No?" His lips twisted into a smirk as he reached over and lifted the pendant from my skin, its faint glow casting eerie shadows across his face. "Then perhaps you can explain why this little trinket emits energy signatures I've only ever seen in the rift."

My stomach tightened, but I kept my expression blank. "It's just a necklace."

"Is it?" Abernathy tilted his head, studying me with the detached curiosity of a man examining an insect. "Then why does it hum every time you're distressed? Why does it react when I activate my machines? And why can't I get it off from around your neck?"

I didn't answer because I didn't know the answers. Since the moment I'd woken up in this time, the pendant had been a mystery—one I was still trying to solve. But even if I had known its secrets, I wouldn't have told him.

Abernathy straightened, his smirk widening. "No matter. I'll figure it out soon enough."

He turned his attention to the machine beside him, flicking a series of switches. The hum grew louder, and the pendant flared, its light pulsing in rhythm with the machine's vibrations.

The pendant burned against my skin, and I clenched my jaw to keep from crying out. I wouldn't give him the satisfaction.

"This is only the beginning," Abernathy said, his voice filled with sick delight. "Once I've unlocked the pendant's full potential, I'll be able to open the rift at will. Imagine it, Miss Williams, entire worlds at my fingertips. Time itself, mine to control."

"You're insane," I spat, my voice shaking despite my best efforts.

"Insane?" He laughed, the sound sharp and grating. "No, my dear. I'm a visionary. And you should feel honored to play a part in my work."

As he turned back to the machine, I allowed myself a single deep breath, forcing my mind to focus. The leather strap on my left arm had loosened just enough for me to wiggle my hand free if I kept at it.

I glanced around the lab, taking in every detail. The machines lined against the walls, their lights blinking in patterns I didn't understand. The shelves were cluttered with tools, papers, and strange artifacts. The glowing case was on the far side of the room, where the Chronarium sat like a shard of molten gold. And Abernathy stood just out of reach, his attention fixed on his work.

I could do this. I had to do this.

Abernathy stepped into my view, his smile as sharp as the scalpel he now held in one hand. "Now…" he said, his tone almost jovial, "… let's see what makes you so special."

The pendant flared as he leaned closer, its hum growing louder. Abernathy paused, his eyes narrowing as he studied it.

"Fascinating," he murmured, reaching for the chain.

"Don't touch it!" I snapped, my voice sharper than I intended.

His gaze flicked to mine, and for a moment, he seemed genuinely curious. "Why not?" he asked, tilting his head.

"Because…" I hesitated, my mind racing. "Because it's unstable. You have no idea what it's capable of."

"Neither do you," he replied, his smile returning. He reached for the pendant again, and I felt a surge of panic. I couldn't let him take it, not when I didn't even fully understand it myself.

"Wait!" I said, my voice trembling. "I'll tell you what you want to know. Just… let me go." Abernathy chuckled, shaking his head.

"Miss Williams. You really think I'd fall for that?" He turned away, moving to one of the machines. "Let's see what this does."

He flipped a switch, and the machine roared to life. The hum of it was deafening, and the pendant responded in kind, its glow intensifying until it was almost blinding. The heat from it seared against my skin, and I cried out despite myself.

Abernathy watched with fascination, his eyes fixed on the pendant as the machine's hum grew louder and louder.

"Yes," he said softly. "Yes, this is it. This is the key."

The straps holding my wrists and ankles vibrated, the energy from the machine coursing through them. My entire body felt like it was on fire, but in the chaos, I noticed something—the vibration was loosening the straps.

Abernathy muttered to himself now, adjusting dials and flipping levers with the precision of a man who thought he was invincible. The machine's hum grew louder, and the pendant's glow intensified, sending a wave of heat through my chest. I gritted my teeth, using the distraction to tug harder at the strap on my wrist.

Finally, my hand slipped free. The relief was

short-lived. I still had my other arm and both legs strapped down, but it was a start. I reached for the nearest tool on the table beside me, my fingers brushing the cool metal of a wrench.

Abernathy didn't notice. He was too busy gloating, his back turned to me.

"You know…" he said, his tone almost conversational, "… I was going to kill you. At the ball, I mean. But then I saw the way you carried yourself, the way you spoke. I thought, *Now, here's someone interesting. Someone worth keeping around.*"

"You flatter me," I said dryly, gripping the wrench tightly.

"Not flattery," he said, glancing over his shoulder. "Observation. You're clever, Miss Williams. But not clever enough to outwit me."

He turned back to the machine, and I struck.

The wrench hit the side of the machine with a loud clang, sending sparks flying. Abernathy spun toward me, his eyes wide with shock as the machine sputtered and groaned.

"What are you—"

Before he could finish, I swung again, this time aiming for the lever that controlled the restraints on the table. The lever snapped off, and the straps around my legs released with a hiss.

I scrambled off the table, my heart pounding as Abernathy lunged for me. I ducked under his arm.

"You little…" Abernathy snarled, grabbing for me again.

I darted toward the shelves, grabbing a glass beaker and hurling it at him. It shattered against his chest, making him stumble back just long enough for me to reach the Chronarium.

The glowing substance in the Chronarium pulsed faintly, its light almost hypnotic. I grabbed the invention, wires sparking as they broke away from it. Then I turned toward the door, my legs shaking beneath me.

"You think you can escape me?" he shouted, lunging toward the machine. "You haven't seen what this technology is capable of!"

He slammed his hand down on a panel of buttons, and the entire room seemed to shift. The air grew heavy, distorting around me like ripples in water. Objects slowed, sped up, and froze in place. The pendant around my neck vibrated violently, almost pulling me backward.

I gritted my teeth, forcing myself to focus. If I could just… I reached for the nearest lever, the metal cold against my palm, and yanked it downward with all my strength. The machine sputtered and groaned, sparks flying as it powered down. The pendant's glow dimmed.

Abernathy spun toward me, his expression furious. "What have you done?" he shouted, lunging toward me.

But I was already running out of the room as my life depended on it.

CHAPTER 15

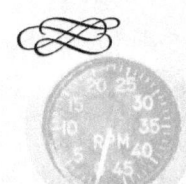

$\mathcal{T}$haddeus

The crash had come from somewhere upstairs, echoing through the cold, silent corridors of Abernathy's workshop. My boots pounded against the polished floors as I sprinted down the hallway, the hum of machinery growing louder with every step.

Closer this time, another sound shattered the quiet—footsteps, fast and erratic.

I rounded the corner just as someone crashed into me.

Evelyn.

She stumbled back, her arms clutching a glowing

case to her chest. Her hair was tangled, her face pale, and her eyes were wild with panic.

"Thaddeus?" She gasped, her voice hoarse and trembling, but before I could respond, she grabbed my arm. "Run!"

Shouting erupted down the corridor behind her. Men's voices. Heavy boots pounded against the floor.

"Stop them!" Abernathy's voice ripped through the chaos, sharp and commanding.

Evelyn's fingers tightened on my arm. "Please!" she begged, her voice breaking. "We have to go!"

I grabbed her wrist and pulled her with me, sprinting down the hallway as fast as I could. The golden glow of the Chronarium in her hands cast warped shadows on the walls as we ran, the echo of our footsteps swallowed by the growing hum of Abernathy's machines.

The mansion was a labyrinth of narrow corridors and locked doors. I tried to piece together the map I'd memorized, but the adrenaline and noise made it impossible to think straight. I glanced back —Evelyn was flagging, her breaths shallow and uneven, her steps faltering.

"Keep going," I urged her, though my lungs burned.

"I-I can't," she choked out, stumbling.

"Yes, you can," I said, pulling her forward and forcing my voice to stay steady. "We're almost there."

It was a lie, but she didn't argue.

The shouting behind us grew louder. I glanced over my shoulder and caught a glimpse of two guards rounding the corner, their weapons glinting in the low light. My stomach twisted.

We turned another corner and hit a dead end.

I looked around frantically. The only way out was a door marked with strange symbols, its edges glowing faintly with the same golden energy as the case in Evelyn's hands.

"No," she whispered, shaking her head. "Not that way. It's unstable."

"We don't have a choice," I said, yanking the door open.

We stumbled into a small storage room, the air thick with the acrid stench of burning metal. Shelves lined the walls, crowded with strange tools and artifacts I didn't recognize.

I bolted the door behind us, my chest heaving as I turned to Evelyn. "Are you all right?"

She nodded shakily, though her face was pale, and her hands trembled as she clutched the case tighter. "Abernathy, he's trying to use the Chronarium and the pendant to open a rift. He wants to visit other timelines and alternate realities.

He doesn't care what it destroys." Her voice cracked.

"You've done well to find this out," I said, though my mind raced with the implications.

The door rattled violently, and I jumped. Someone was trying to break it down.

"Step away, Miss Williams!" Abernathy's voice came from the other side, cold and venomous. "You can't outrun me. You can't stop this. You have no idea what you're holding."

Evelyn flinched, her fingers tightening around the case. She didn't say a word, but the fear in her eyes was matched only by the determination that hadn't left her since the moment I'd found her.

"Stay behind me," I said, grabbing a crowbar from one of the shelves.

The door burst open, and Abernathy strode into the room, flanked by two guards. He looked utterly composed as if he weren't the one chasing us through his damn mansion.

"Thaddeus," he drawled, his lip curling. "I should have known you'd come crawling after her."

"Abernathy," I spat, positioning myself between him and Evelyn. "Let us go."

He ignored me, his cold eyes fixed on Evelyn. "You don't even know what you're holding, do you?" he said, gesturing to the glowing case. "The

Chronarium isn't just a tool. It's a key. A bridge. And you two..." His gaze lingered on Evelyn, calculating and cruel. "You're just collateral."

I didn't wait for him to finish. I lunged at the nearest guard, swinging the crowbar hard. It connected with a sickening crack, and the man crumpled, but the second guard was already moving. He tackled me, slamming me against the shelves, and I grunted as the air was knocked from my lungs.

"Thaddeus!" Evelyn screamed, her voice raw with panic.

I shoved the guard off me and swung again, catching him in the ribs. He staggered, but Abernathy had already moved. He grabbed Evelyn by the arm, yanking her toward him.

"No!" I shouted, throwing myself at him.

The impact sent us both crashing to the floor. The case slipped from Evelyn's hands, clattering loudly against the floor. The glowing Chronarium inside pulsed violently, the light growing brighter, hotter.

"Evelyn, grab it!" I shouted, struggling to pin Abernathy down.

She hesitated, her hands shaking as she reached for the case. But Abernathy shoved me off with a surprising burst of strength, sending me sprawling. He lunged for Evelyn, his hand outstretched.

I didn't think. I grabbed the first thing I could reach—a heavy metal pipe—and swung it at Abernathy's legs. He went down with a snarl, and I scrambled to my feet, grabbing Evelyn's arm.

"Run!" I yelled, dragging her toward the door.

We bolted down the hallway, the glow of the Chronarium lighting the way as the sound of Abernathy's furious shouts faded behind us.

We burst into the warming light of the day, stumbling onto the gravel path that led away from the mansion. For a moment, the only sounds were our ragged breathing and the distant hum of Abernathy's machines.

Evelyn clung to the case, her entire body trembling. "Thaddeus..." she began, but her voice gave out.

I pulled her close, my eyes scanning the dark landscape around us. Home right now felt like miles away.

CHAPTER 16

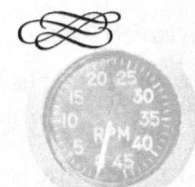

*E*velyn

The last thing I remembered was the glow of the Chronarium in my arms and Thaddeus's voice urging me forward. The night air was cold against my skin, and it told me that we had been hiding for the day, but I couldn't remember as my mind slipped in and out of consciousness. My head pounded, and every step felt like a battle.

"Almost there," he said, though I could hear the strain in his voice.

The rest blurred—the crunch of gravel underfoot, the creak of a door opening, and the warmth of somewhere safe. My knees buckled, and before I could hit the ground, strong arms caught me.

"I've got you," Thaddeus said, his voice low and soothing.

I wanted to tell him I was fine, that I could walk, but my body betrayed me. I slumped against his chest, too weak to protest. He lifted me effortlessly, his arms steady as he carried me through the dimly lit halls of his mansion. The scent of oil and metal clung to him, mixed with something warmer, something distinctly him.

The world tilted as I rested my head against his shoulder, my breath shallow but steady. I could hear the faint hum of his machines in the distance, but it was his heartbeat—strong and steady—that kept me grounded.

"Evelyn?" a familiar voice called out, and I blinked, catching sight of Clara rushing toward us. Her eyes flicked to Thaddeus, then back to me, her expression softening with concern.

"She needs water," Thaddeus said, his tone clipped but not unkind.

Clara nodded, her skirts swishing as she hurried away.

Thaddeus carried me into a room—my room, I realized. The bed was still unmade from the last time I'd been there, and the faint scent of lavender lingered in the air. He gently lowered me onto the mattress, his hands lingering for a moment as if to make sure I wouldn't collapse further.

"I'm fine," I managed to whisper, though my voice sounded far weaker than I intended.

"You're not," he said, his sharp gaze scanning me for injuries. "Stay still."

Clara returned with a glass, along with a basin of water and a clean cloth, setting them down on the bedside table. She hesitated for a moment, her eyes flicking between the two of us.

"I'll leave you to it," she said softly, a knowing look passing between her and Thaddeus. Then she slipped out of the room, closing the door behind her with a quiet click.

Thaddeus pulled up a chair beside the bed and helped me to sip the water. Then he dipped the cloth into the basin, wringing it out before turning back to me. His movements were precise, almost mechanical, but there was a tenderness to them that made my chest ache.

"This might sting," he said, his voice softer now.

"I can handle it," I replied, though I wasn't sure if I was trying to convince him or myself.

He pressed the cloth to the cut on my temple, and I winced, the sharp sting bringing tears to my eyes. He paused, his brows furrowing.

"Sorry," he murmured, his thumb brushing against my cheek in a gesture so gentle it made my heart skip a beat.

"It's fine," I said, my voice barely above a whisper.

He continued to clean the wound, his touch careful and thoughtful. I studied his face as he worked—the hard lines of his jaw, the faint filagree on the metal that made his cheeks. I'd seen him angry, determined, even frantic. But this was different.

When he finally set the cloth aside, his gaze met mine, and the air between us shifted.

"Evelyn," he said, my name a low rumble that sent a shiver down my spine.

I didn't know who moved first, but suddenly, his lips were on mine, warm and insistent. Everything else fell away—the ache in my body, the weight of the Chronarium, the danger we'd just escaped. All that mattered was him.

I threaded my fingers through his hair, pulling him closer as the kiss deepened. His hands cradled my face, his touch firm but reverent as if I might break beneath him. Heat pooled in my core, and for the first time in what felt like forever, I let myself forget the rest of the world.

His lips trailed down to my jaw, then to the sensitive spot just below my ear, and I couldn't stop the soft gasp that escaped me. My body arched toward him, desperate to close the space between us, but the moment I felt his hand slide down to my waist, I froze.

He stopped immediately, pulling back just enough to meet my gaze.

"What's wrong?" he asked, his voice low and rough.

I opened my mouth to speak, but the words caught in my throat. My cheeks burned, and I looked away, embarrassed.

"Evelyn," he said again, his tone softer now, coaxing. "Talk to me."

"I haven't..." The words trembled on the edge of my lips. I forced them out, barely audible. "I haven't done this before."

The admission hung in the air between us, raw and exposed. My cheeks burned, the heat crawling down my neck as I looked away, unable to meet his gaze. I felt small like a child fumbling with something far beyond her grasp.

I bit my lip, trying to will away the wave of shame that rose in my chest. It wasn't like I'd never had the chance—there'd been boys, sure. But I was always more interested in books than kisses, in learning than lingering touches. And then, life happened. The kind of life that didn't leave room for softness. Somewhere along the way, I'd convinced myself I didn't need or want it, that I was fine on my own.

But here, with Thaddeus, it was different. He wasn't even fully human, and yet that didn't matter. I didn't care about the metal and wires, the patches of machinery woven into his body. All I cared about was the way he made me feel when he looked at me, like I was someone worth fighting for and saving.

So why couldn't I push past the knot of nerves tightening in my chest?

For a moment, he didn't respond, and the silence pressed down on me like a heavy weight. I risked a glance at him, bracing myself for judgment or pity. But his expression was unreadable, his blue eyes searching mine as if trying to piece together the puzzle of my hesitation.

Then, his hand came up, and I flinched slightly, almost imperceptibly. But he noticed. His movements slowed, calculated, and careful as though he were approaching something fragile. When his hand finally cupped my cheek, his thumb brushed against my skin with a tenderness that made my heart ache.

"You don't have to explain," he said quietly, his voice steady but warm. "Not to me."

The words hit me harder than I expected. My throat tightened, and I blinked back the sting of tears. I shook my head, my voice breaking when I spoke. "I just... I don't want to disappoint you."

"You couldn't," he said immediately, the conviction in his tone leaving no room for doubt.

I wanted to believe him, but the knot in my chest only tightened. "It's not just that," I admitted, my voice barely above a whisper. "It's... everything. I've spent so long shutting this part of myself down, pretending it didn't matter. And now, with you..." I trailed off, struggling to put the chaos in my head into words.

His thumb stilled on my cheek, his gaze softening. "Now it matters."

I nodded, swallowing hard. "It matters too much. And that scares me."

He was quiet for a long moment, the weight of his hand grounding me, keeping me from spiraling. Then he leaned closer, his forehead resting against mine.

"It's okay to be scared," he murmured. "But you don't have to rush this. Not with me."

I closed my eyes, his warmth chasing away some of the cold fear that had taken root inside me. "You must think I'm ridiculous," I whispered, a bitter laugh escaping me.

"Ridiculous?" His voice was low, almost a growl, and when I opened my eyes, I found him staring at me with such intensity that it made my breath hitch. "Evelyn, you're the bravest person I've ever met. And trust me, I've met a lot of people."

My lips curved into a small, shaky smile. "You really mean that?"

He nodded, his hand slipping from my cheek to trail gently down my arm, his touch leaving a warmth that lingered. "Every word." His next words were softer but no less certain. "I'll wait. Until you're ready."

A pang of frustration welled in my chest, mingling with the ache of wanting him so badly it hurt. I shook my head, my fingers curling into the fabric of his shirt, desperate to hold onto him.

"I am ready," I said, but the tremble in my voice gave me away.

"You're tense," he said simply, his eyes searching mine.

I bit my lip, frustrated by how easily he saw through me. "It's just..." I trailed off, unsure how to explain the nervous knot in my stomach.

He seemed to understand anyway.

"Evelyn..." he said softly, his tone low and coaxing, "... look at me."

Slowly, I lifted my eyes to meet his, my breath hitching at the intensity in his blue gaze. He held my stare for a moment, steady and unyielding before his hands moved to the buttons of his shirt. Each movement was purposeful, almost reverent as if he were peeling back more than just fabric.

My heart pounded as the shirt slipped from his shoulders, revealing the intricate blend of flesh and metal beneath. His chest was broad and powerful, the muscles sculpted and firm, but it was the patches of gleaming steel that drew my attention. They caught the dim light, their edges melding seamlessly with his skin as though the machine and the man had always been one.

The faint hum of his mechanical parts wasn't cold or lifeless—it was steady, rhythmic, almost alive. The metal didn't detract from him—it was part of him, seamlessly intertwined with the strength of his flesh. He wasn't a patchwork creation. He was something more than human, something extraordinary. And it made him beautiful in a way I hadn't expected.

Faint scars crisscrossed the human parts of him —some faded, others newer—and I found myself wondering about the stories they held. My fingers twitched with the urge to touch him, to trace the lines of his body and feel the metal's coolness against my skin.

"This is me," he said quietly, his voice tinged with vulnerability. "All of me."

I couldn't speak. My gaze drifted lower, taking in the sharp lines of his abdomen, where metal and muscle intertwined like a work of art. The faint hum of his mechanical parts reached my ears, a subtle reminder of the complexity of the man standing before me.

Then my gaze traveled farther down, and my breath hitched sharply in my throat. He was hard beneath his trousers, the unmistakable outline of his arousal straining against the fabric. Heat bloomed in my cheeks, spreading like wildfire through my body, leaving me dizzy and breathless. My pulse thundered in my ears, and my skin felt impossibly warm as if his gaze alone had set me on fire.

My fingers twitched at my sides, aching with the urge to reach for him, to trace the sharp lines of his metal and feel the strength of the man beneath the machine. But my body felt frozen in place, caught between the knot of nerves tightening in my stomach and the growing ache of desire that was impossible to ignore.

He stood there, unflinching, letting me see him—not just the mechanical parts or the flesh, but the man beneath it all. That openness, that willingness to expose all of himself to me, struck something deep inside. My chest tightened, and my heart hammered like a relentless drum.

I'd been afraid of him once—that first moment I saw him, all sharp edges and glowing eyes. He'd looked like something out of a nightmare, a machine built only for destruction. But now, standing here, bare and unguarded, he wasn't a monster. He was a man who had fought for, carried, and cared for me. And I realized, with a clarity that stole my breath, that I didn't just trust him. I wanted him.

His hands moved to his belt, the soft sound of leather slipping through the hooks making the tension inside me coil tighter. My breath quickened as he unfastened his trousers, unbuttoning them with measured care. When he pushed them down, my heart stopped for a moment before thundering so loudly I was sure he could hear it.

His cock sprang free, thick and hard, his arousal leaving no question of what he wanted. My breath stuttered as my eyes took him in, the sheer intimacy of the moment leaving me both overwhelmed and entranced. He looked human, at least the parts that mattered. His cock, his balls—they were flesh, familiar, and real, no different from any man, and yet there was something more. Something uniquely him.

Any lingering fear, the quiet, nagging voice in the back of my head whispering doubts about what he was, human or something else, fled. The sight of him standing there, bare and unguarded, silenced every question and hesitation. He wasn't a monster. He wasn't a machine. He was himself, and that was all I needed to know.

And yet, even now, with his body exposed and his desire laid bare, he was holding back, denying me. Not because he didn't want me but because he wanted to be sure I was ready. The weight of that realization swept over me, shaking me to my core.

"I want you to see me," he said, his voice low and steady, though there was a rawness to it that made my pulse quicken. "And I want you to know that when we do this... when you're ready... it'll be because you want to. Not because you feel like you have to."

His words washed over me, grounding me even as my emotions churned. The nervous knot in my stomach mixed with a growing ache of desire, the two battling for control. He was more than I'd ever imagined—strong, vulnerable, human, and something entirely his own—and I wanted him.

But the truth was, I wasn't sure if I wanted him enough to silence the voice in my head whispering that I wasn't ready.

I swallowed hard, my heart pounding in my chest. "I do want to," I whispered.

He leaned forward, brushing a soft kiss against

my lips. "Not yet," he murmured against my mouth, his hands cradling my face. "You're still not ready."

I wanted to argue, to tell him I could handle it, but the truth was written all over me. My body was tense, my mind a whirlwind of nerves and desire.

He pulled back slightly, resting his forehead against mine. "We'll get there," he said softly. "But not tonight."

I nodded, my cheeks burning as I let myself relax against him. For the first time in days, I felt safe.

CHAPTER 17

*E*velyn

The pendant felt heavier in my trembling hands, its faint glow flickering weakly like a dying ember. I tightened my grip despite the sharp ache in my wrists, desperate to steady it. Beside me, the Chronarium pulsed faintly on the workbench, its swirling gold energy teasing us with potential.

"Come on," I muttered under my breath, holding the pendant closer and willing it to do something. "Work, dammit."

Nothing.

"It glowed brighter when I was holding it. Just for a moment," I said, my voice quiet.

"It's not going to activate like this." Thaddeus's voice was calm but carried an edge of impatience. He stepped closer, his towering frame casting a shadow over the workbench.

"Then how is it supposed to activate?" I snapped, the frustration boiling over. "We've done everything to combine the pendant and the Chronarium, aligned the energy fields. Why isn't it working?"

"Maybe there's a failsafe," he said after a long moment, his tone distant as he focused on the pendant that hung around my neck, nestled between my breasts. The memory of him naked caused me to flush, and I quickly pushed it aside.

"Abernathy was paranoid. He wouldn't have made it simple. There's something we're missing," Thaddeus said, rubbing his temples.

I let my head fall back against the chair, closing my eyes and willing the pounding in my skull to subside. "We don't have time to figure this out," I said quietly.

"We'll make time," he said firmly.

I opened my eyes to find him watching me, his sharp, angular features tense with determination. It was the kind of look that could have been reassuring if it hadn't also reminded me of how much he was carrying—the weight of this mission, the responsibility of keeping me safe.

I sighed, flexing my sore wrists and wincing at the sharp sting. He noticed immediately.

"Let me see," he said, stepping closer.

"I'm fine," I lied, but he didn't listen.

Before I could protest, he was kneeling in front of me, his hands reaching for mine with a gentleness that caught me off guard. He took my wrists carefully, his touch light but firm as he studied the grazes left by Abernathy's restraints.

"You're not fine," he said quietly, his voice softer now. His thumbs brushed over the tender skin, sending a shiver up my spine. "You've been pushing yourself too hard."

I swallowed hard, my throat suddenly dry. "We don't exactly have the luxury of taking it easy."

He didn't respond right away, his focus still on my wrists, his touch lingering. The warmth of his flesh hand contrasted with the coolness of his metal one, the combination unexpectedly soothing. His metal fingers were surprisingly delicate against my torn skin, and for a moment, I forgot about the pain altogether. My breath caught as his thumbs brushed over the tender spots, the quiet, heavier tension between us making me bite the inside of my cheek to keep from shivering.

"You need to rest," he said finally, his voice barely above a whisper.

I wanted to argue, but the exhaustion in my body and the sincerity in his eyes stopped me. I nodded reluctantly, letting my hands fall to my lap as he stood.

As he turned back to the workbench, I couldn't help but watch him. There was an urgency to his movements and a tension in his shoulders that hadn't been there before.

"What if we can't figure this out?" I asked, my voice breaking the heavy silence.

He didn't look at me as he sorted through Abernathy's scattered notes, but I saw his jaw tighten. "We will."

"But what if we don't?" I pressed, unable to stop the flood of doubt from spilling out. "What if Abernathy comes for us before we're ready? What if we're already too late?"

He stopped, his hand hovering over one of the pages. When he finally turned to face me, his expression was unreadable, his blue eyes glinting in the dim light.

"Then we fight," he said simply.

For a split second, his jaw tightened, and I caught a flicker of something in his eyes—doubt, maybe fear. But then it was gone, replaced by the unshakable determination that had carried us this far. "And we don't stop until we win."

The certainty in his voice should have been comforting, but instead, it made my chest ache. He was so willing to throw himself into danger, so determined to shoulder the burden alone.

He turned back to the notes before I could respond, muttering something under his breath as he scanned one of his old journals from when Abernathy funded his inventions.

He pointed to a section of the notes. "Abernathy mentioned something about a 'sacrifice of intent.' It's vague, but it seems to be tied to the pendant's activation."

"A sacrifice of intent?" I repeated, frowning. "What does that even mean?"

"I'm not sure," he admitted, his brow furrowing. "But it suggests that the pendant doesn't just respond to energy. It's tied to the user's will, their emotions, memories, something deeply personal, probably your heritage, but we have established that."

I stared at the pendant, lifting it from where it nestled on my chest, the faint glow barely visible now. "When we were escaping…" I hesitated, the memory flickering in my mind. "It glowed brighter when I was holding it. Just for a moment."

Thaddeus turned to me sharply. "What were you thinking about?"

"I don't know," I said, trying to recall. "I was scared. I was thinking about getting out, about surviving. About..." My voice trailed off as I realized the truth. "About you."

His eyes widened slightly, but he said nothing. The silence stretched between us, heavy and charged.

The moment was broken by the sound of hurried footsteps. Clara burst into the room, her face pale with fear.

"They're coming," she said, her voice trembling. "Abernathy's men. They must have tracked the pendant's energy signature."

Thaddeus cursed under his breath. "We need to leave. Now."

I stood, ignoring the pull on my ankles where the restraints had been. "Where do we go?"

"Anywhere but here," he said, already moving toward the door. "Clara, pack whatever you can carry. Evelyn, stay close to me."

Before I could respond, a deafening explosion rocked the mansion. The floor trembled beneath my feet, and I stumbled, grabbing the workbench for support.

"They're already here," Thaddeus growled, his hand going to the pistol at his side.

The sound of shattering glass and splintering

wood echoed through the halls, followed by the heavy thud of approaching footsteps. My heart pounded as I looked to Thaddeus, his face set in grim determination.

"Stay behind me," he said, his voice calm but deadly.

And then the door burst open.

CHAPTER 18

*T*haddeus

The door shattered inward with an ear-splitting crash, splinters of wood scattering across the room. I stepped in front of Evelyn instinctively, my body moving before my mind could process the assault. Three figures stormed in, their faces obscured by dark masks, weapons gleaming in the dim light.

"Stay behind me," I barked, drawing my pistol.

Evelyn didn't respond, but I felt her shift closer to my back. Good. For now, she was listening.

The first man lunged. I fired once, the shot precise, and he crumpled to the floor. The second moved faster, sidestepping my aim and swinging a crowbar at my head. I ducked, the air hissing as the metal arced past me.

The third man hesitated, his gaze flicking to Evelyn.

Bad move.

I surged forward, slamming my metal fist into his chest. The force sent him sprawling into the wall with a sickening thud. He didn't get back up.

The second man came at me again, his movements erratic, desperate. I caught his wrist mid-swing, the crowbar clattering to the floor. My other hand curled into a tight fist, and I drove it into his jaw. He went down hard, his body limp before he hit the floor.

The room fell silent except for the sharp, shallow breaths coming from behind me.

"Are you okay?" I asked, turning to Evelyn.

She nodded, but her wide eyes betrayed her fear. "I'm fine," she said, though her voice trembled.

More footsteps echoed from outside—heavy, purposeful. They weren't done with us yet.

"Come on," I said, grabbing her hand. "We need to move."

We sprinted through the workshop, weaving between scattered tools and half-finished machines. I could hear the others closing in, their voices sharp and commanding. I always had a backdoor, one I never thought I'd use.

I pushed the heavy wooden door, opening into a hidden passage, a narrow, dimly lit corridor that twisted and turned in ways only I could truly navigate.

"This will slow them down," I muttered, glancing back to make sure Evelyn was still behind me. The pounding of boots echoed ominously in the narrow passage.

"Clara... the others..." she gasped, her breath catching in her throat as she stumbled over the uneven stones.

"There's a safe room," I said, my voice clipped. "They know where to go."

"I hope they make it," she whispered, her voice laced with fear.

The passage opened abruptly into a cavernous storage room filled with looming shadows and the skeletal remains of rusting machinery. I stopped, my breath coming in ragged gasps, and turned to Evelyn. "We can't stay here. They'll find us."

"What's the plan?" she asked, her voice steadier now.

I hesitated. Truthfully, I didn't have one. The attack had come too fast, too sudden. We weren't ready for this.

"We need to get the pendant and Chronarium out of here," I said, my voice low and urgent. "If they get their hands on it—"

"They won't," I cut her off, my grip tightening on the pendant. "I won't let it happen."

A sudden screech of metal ripped through the air. The main door buckled inward, exploding in a shower of sparks and smoke. I instinctively shielded Evelyn with my body, coughing against the acrid fumes. A figure emerged from the swirling chaos, impossibly tall and menacing.

Abernathy.

His dark coat billowed around him like a shroud, his eyes, cold and predatory, fixed on mine. He was taller than I remembered, his presence radiating a chilling aura of power.

"Thaddeus," he greeted, his voice a smooth, mocking purr. "You've been a busy little automaton. But you should have known better than to try and hide from me."

I stepped in front of Evelyn, my hand instinctively going to the pistol at my hip. "Stay back," I warned, my voice tight.

A low chuckle rumbled in Abernathy's chest. "Still playing the hero? Such a tiresome charade."

"You won't get what you came for," I growled, my control fraying at the edges.

His gaze flicked to Evelyn, a predatory gleam in his eyes. Before I could react, his hand snapped up, revealing a small, humming device—the Chronarium. The air shimmered, distorting around him, the hum intensifying into a high-pitched whine.

"Thaddeus," Evelyn whispered, her voice tight with panic.

I grabbed her arm, pulling her behind me as the device in Abernathy's hand flared to life. A jagged tear appeared in the air, its edges shimmering with unstable energy. The rift crackled and pulsed, sending waves of heat and cold through the room.

"You see, Thaddeus..." Abernathy said, his tone almost gleeful, "... you've been playing with forces you don't understand. But I do. And now..." He gestured to the rift, his eyes gleaming. "Now, I'll show you what true power looks like."

The rift expanded, its energy surging outward and tearing through the room. Machinery groaned and buckled under the strain, and the floor beneath us cracked.

"Evelyn, run!" I shouted, shoving her toward the far door.

"What about you?" she yelled, her eyes wide with fear.

"Go!" I barked, firing a shot at Abernathy to keep him distracted.

She hesitated for only a moment before turning and sprinting toward the exit. I followed, keeping my body between her and the chaos.

The rift's energy lashed out, striking the wall beside me and sending shards of stone flying. I stumbled but forced myself to keep moving, my focus fixed on Evelyn as she reached the door.

"Thaddeus!" she called, holding it open for me.

I reached her just as the room behind us collapsed, the rift consuming everything in its path.

We tumbled into the hallway, the door slamming shut behind us. The sound of destruction echoed from the other side, but we didn't stop.

We ran.

Later that night, we had escaped and found shelter in a small, abandoned cabin in the country-side south of London, staring at the floor as Evelyn paced restlessly nearby.

"This isn't your fault," she said, her voice cutting through the silence as she sat in the corner.

I didn't look at her. "Yes, it is. I should've been faster. Smarter. I should've stopped him. He has the Chronarium again."

"But not the pendant, and you can't do every-thing alone," she said, her tone softer now.

I finally met her gaze, the intensity in her eyes

catching me off guard. "And if I lose you?" I asked, the words slipping out before I could stop them.

She froze, her expression softening. "You won't."

For a moment, the tension between us hung heavily in the air. Then she stepped closer, her hand brushing mine.

"We'll get it back," she said quietly.

As the night wore on, we began outlining a plan to track Abernathy. Despite my doubts, I couldn't bring myself to argue. We had to bring the fight to him.

We had no choice. If we didn't stop him, no one would.

And this time, I wouldn't let him win.

CHAPTER 19

*E*velyn

The observatory loomed ahead, its silhouette stark against the stormy sky. The jagged remains of its once-pristine dome jutted out like broken teeth, and a strange, pulsing light emanated from within. It wasn't natural, that light. It flickered and pulsed, a cold, otherworldly glow that tightened my chest.

"We're close," Thaddeus said, his voice low but steady.

The wind howled around us as we climbed the crumbling steps to the entrance. The pendant's surface was warm against my skin, and my dress was low-cut to show it off. Even now, it seemed to react to the energy radiating from the observatory, glowing faintly in response to the chaotic rift inside.

"Do you feel that?" I asked, glancing at Thaddeus.

He nodded, his metal hand flexing at his side. "Time's unraveling here. We need to be careful."

We stepped inside, and the air instantly changed. It felt heavier, like walking through water, and the faint hum of the rift vibrated in my skull. The observatory walls were cracked and scorched, but worse than the damage was the way the space itself seemed... wrong.

The hallway ahead twisted impossibly, bending at angles that defied logic. Shadows moved where there shouldn't have been light, and as we walked, I caught glimpses of things.

A flash of myself, running down the same hallway but wearing different clothes. A shadowy figure standing at the edge of my vision was gone when I turned my head. And the voices, soft whispers that sounded like Thaddeus and me.

"This place is a nightmare," I muttered, my voice shaky.

"It's the rift," Thaddeus said, his jaw tight. "It's destabilizing everything... time, space, memory. Don't trust anything you see."

We pressed on, navigating the warped corridors as the rift's energy grew stronger. The air felt heavier with every step, and the walls around us seemed to pulse faintly as if alive. Eventually, we reached a room that stretched endlessly before us, its floor a gleaming black void that made my stomach twist. The only way across was a narrow, spiraling metal staircase, impossibly suspended in midair, its edges flickering like a mirage.

I froze, staring at the staircase. The air around it shimmered, distorting the edges of the steps in a way that made them seem almost intangible. "Wait," I said, holding out a hand to stop Thaddeus.

He turned to me, his brow furrowed. "What is it?"

"The distortion," I said, pointing to the faint ripples that danced along the outer edges of the steps. "It's stronger there. If we stick to the middle of the staircase, we might avoid whatever's making it unstable."

Thaddeus studied it for a moment, his blue eyes scanning the shimmering air. Then he nodded, his expression tight. "Good catch. Stay close."

He stepped onto the staircase first, his movements steady and deliberate. I followed close behind, gripping the railing tightly, my heart pounding as the steps creaked faintly beneath us. The air shimmered like heat waves, and for a moment, the world around me shifted.

I gasped as flashes of another time appeared—

people in lab coats bustling around the observatory, machines whirring, voices echoing with urgency. The scene flickered like an old film reel, distorted and incomplete, before vanishing as quickly as it had come. Only the eerie silence and the faint hum of the rift remained.

"You okay?" Thaddeus asked, glancing back at me.

I nodded, though my grip on the railing tightened. "Yeah. Let's keep going."

We moved cautiously, keeping to the center of the steps as the air continued to shimmer around us. Despite the distortion, the staircase held firm beneath our weight, and after what felt like an eternity, we finally reached the other side, but the disorientation left me dizzy. Thaddeus steadied me with one hand, his touch grounding me.

The deeper we went, the worse the distortions became. Rooms shifted and stretched, doors appeared and disappeared, and time itself seemed to loop in on itself. At one point, I saw the two of us in the distance, walking in the opposite direction.

"Don't look at them," Thaddeus warned, his grip firm as he pulled me forward, away from the flickering figures.

We pressed on, the warped corridors twisting and shifting around us. Each step seemed harder than the last, the air growing heavier, pressing against my chest like an invisible weight. The walls pulsed faintly as if alive, their surfaces rippling in sync with the low hum of the rift.

Finally, we reached a small alcove, a brief respite from the chaos. I leaned against the wall, trying to catch my breath.

"We're close to the central chamber," Thaddeus said, his voice low. "Abernathy will be there."

I looked at him, and for the first time, I noticed how tense he was. His shoulders were rigid, his jaw clenched, and his hands—one flesh, one metal—were curled into tight fists.

"Thaddeus," I said softly, stepping closer. "Are you okay?"

He exhaled sharply, running a hand through his hair. "I don't know," he admitted. "This place... it's pulling at everything. Memories. Regrets. Doubts. It's like it knows exactly where to hit to hurt me."

I placed a hand on his arm, the warmth of his skin a stark contrast to the cold, metallic surface of his other limb. "You're not doing this alone," I said firmly.

His eyes met mine, and for a moment, the weight of everything seemed to lift. "You always do that," he murmured.

"Do what?"

"Make me believe I'm not completely lost."

The intensity in his gaze sent a shiver down my spine. The space around us seemed to blur, the distorted reality of the observatory fading into the background. It was just us now—two people standing on the edge of something massive, something that could destroy everything.

"Thaddeus..." I began, but my words caught in my throat as he stepped closer.

His hand cupped my cheek, his touch gentle despite the urgency of the moment. "If we don't make it out of this..." he said, his voice low and rough, "... there's something you need to know."

I swallowed hard, my heart pounding. "What?"

He hesitated, his eyes searching mine. Then, as if the words weren't enough, he kissed me.

It wasn't soft or tentative. It was desperate, a collision of fear, longing, and everything we'd been holding back. His hand tangled in my hair, pulling me closer, and I pressed against him, losing myself in the heat of the moment.

The world around us seemed to vanish, the distortions of the observatory replaced by his steady, grounding presence. His metal arm wrapped around my waist, its coolness a stark contrast to the warmth of his lips.

I didn't want it to end, but the hum of the rift

grew louder, a sharp reminder of the danger we were still in.

"We should—" I started, pulling back slightly.

"I know," he said, his voice hoarse.

For a moment, we just stood there, our foreheads pressed together, breathing heavily. The connection between us felt fragile and bittersweet like a thread stretched taut.

"We'll finish this," he said, his voice steady again. "And then…"

"And then," I echoed, my chest aching with everything left unsaid and undone.

We stepped back into the chaos of the observatory, our resolve hardened.

The central chamber was a scene of pure madness. The rift pulsed in the center, a swirling vortex of light and shadow that seemed to consume everything around it. Abernathy stood at the edge, the Chronarium glowing in his hands as he fed its energy into the rift.

"You're too late," Abernathy said, his voice echoing unnaturally, blending with the pulsing hum of the rift behind him.

"No," Thaddeus said firmly, stepping forward.

Abernathy tilted his head, his smirk deepening. "Do you see it, Thaddeus?" he asked, gesturing toward the swirling chaos of the rift. "The power to rewrite everything. To tear apart this broken world and build something new."

"You're going to destroy everything," Thaddeus shot back, his voice sharp, cutting through the drone of the rift.

Abernathy barked out a laugh, wild and unhinged. His eyes glinted with feverish excitement as he stepped closer to the swirling vortex. "Destroy? No. This world is already broken, it's fractured beyond repair." He turned to face us fully, the rift's light casting eerie shadows across his face. "But the rift? It holds the power to undo every failure, every mistake. I'll reshape time itself and erase the pain, the loss, the regrets. I'll make it perfect."

His voice rose, growing louder and more desperate with every word, his hands outstretched as if he could grasp the chaotic energy of the rift itself. "You don't understand, Thaddeus. This isn't destruction. It's salvation."

"You can't control it," Thaddeus shot back, his voice sharp.

Abernathy laughed, a wild, unhinged sound. "Control it? I am it."

The rift surged, its energy lashing out and tearing through the chamber. The floor beneath us cracked, and I stumbled, barely catching myself.

"Evelyn!" Thaddeus shouted, grabbing my arm and pulling me back from the edge.

Abernathy raised the Chronarium high, its energy flaring. "Say goodbye to this timeline," he said, his voice triumphant.

The rift exploded outward, and everything went white.

CHAPTER 20

*T*haddeus

The light from the rift was blinding, a searing, chaotic pulse that seemed to tear at the edges of reality itself. My ears rang with the sound of its energy, a low, resonant hum that vibrated in my chest and threatened to pull me apart. I forced myself to focus, to push past the overwhelming noise and light because Evelyn was still beside me, and if I faltered now, we'd both be lost.

"Thaddeus!" Evelyn's voice cut through the chaos, sharp and clear. She gripped the pendant tightly, its golden glow flickering like a fading star. "It's not enough! The Chronarium... he's still feeding it into the rift!"

I followed her gaze to where Abernathy stood at the edge of the swirling vortex. The Chronarium floated in his outstretched hand, its energy pouring into the rift like a golden river. His face was illuminated by the light, his expression one of pure, unhinged triumph.

"You can't stop this!" he shouted, his voice echoing unnaturally as the rift twisted the air around him. "This is the future! The past! Everything! I am time itself!"

He wasn't human anymore. The rift's energy was consuming him, his form flickering and distorting like a broken projection. But he didn't care. He didn't see the madness in his reflection, he only saw the power.

"Evelyn," I said, grabbing her arm and pulling her back as another surge of energy lashed out, cracking the floor beneath our feet. "We need to get the Chronarium away from him. Without it, the rift might stabilize."

"How?" she shouted, her voice trembling with anger and fear. "We can't get near him! That thing will tear us apart!"

"The pendant," I said, my mind racing. "It's connected to the rift. It's why he was so desperate to get it back. It has the same energy as the Chronarium. If we use it to disrupt the flow…"

Her eyes widened as she realized what I was saying. "It could work."

"It has to," I said, though doubt gnawed at the edges of my confidence. "But there's one problem. The pendant needs intent. Focus. A connection to its energy."

The words echoed in my mind, *a sacrifice of intent.*

"I'll do it," I said, the decision coming as quickly as the words. "I'll use the pendant."

Her head snapped toward me, her expression sharp with disbelief. "No."

"Evelyn, listen to me—"

"No," she said again, stepping closer, her voice firm despite the turmoil around us. "You don't get to make that decision alone."

"It's not a decision," I said, my voice rising. "It's the only way. You saw what Abernathy became. The rift consumes people. If anyone's going to take that risk, it's me."

"Why? Because you think you're expendable?" she snapped, her eyes blazing with anger. "Because you're more machine than man? Don't you dare, Thaddeus. Don't you dare think you're any less human than I am."

Her words hit harder than any blow I'd ever taken. I opened my mouth to argue, but the look in her eyes stopped me.

"You've spent your whole life inventing," she said, her voice softening. "But you don't have to do this alone. That's the only way this works."

I stared at her, the chaos of the rift fading into the background for a moment. Her determination and fire were unshakable. She wasn't going to let me shut her out, not this time.

"Fine," I relented.

We stepped toward the rift, the heat and energy pressing against us like a gale-force wind. The pendant glowed brighter, its light pushing back against the darkness. I placed my hand over hers, the cool metal of my fingers brushing against her warm skin.

"Focus," I said, my voice steady despite the storm raging around us. "Think of everything we're fighting for. Everything we've lost. Everything we want to save."

Her eyes met mine, and in that moment, I felt it— the connection. The fear, the hope, the unspoken emotions that had been building between us since this all began. It was raw and overwhelming, surging through the pendant like a current.

The rift screamed in response, its energy

thrashing wildly as the pendant's light grew brighter. Abernathy turned toward us, his expression twisting from triumph to rage.

"No!" he shouted, his voice distorted. "You don't understand! You'll destroy everything!"

"You've already done that," Evelyn shot back, her voice strong and defiant.

The pendant flared, its light engulfing us both. I felt its energy course through me, pulling at every part of who I was—my memories, regrets, and hopes. It wasn't just power. It was us.

"No!" I shouted, suddenly realizing what she was going to do.

She broke the chain holding the pendant around her neck and thrust it into the rift. The pendant was her only way home. I didn't mean she should sacrifice her future.

The light was blinding, a searing pulse that seemed to freeze time itself. Abernathy screamed, his form disintegrating as the rift's energy turned on him, pulling him into its void. His final cry echoed for an instant before silence fell.

The rift shrank, its chaotic energy collapsing in on itself. The Chronarium shattered, its golden glow fading into nothingness.

And then it was over.

The observatory was silent, the air still and

heavy. I looked at Evelyn, her face pale and streaked with tears, but her eyes were steady.

"You did it," I said, my voice barely above a whisper. I couldn't bring myself to say that she could never go home again. This woman was something else, stronger than me, for certain, and I was in awe of her.

"We did it," she corrected, a faint smile tugging at her lips.

For a moment, the weight of everything lifted. We had survived. The rift was gone, and Abernathy with it. But as I looked at the shattered remains of the Chronarium, a new unease settled over me.

"What if it's not over?" I said, voicing the thought that had been gnawing at me.

Evelyn stepped closer, her hand brushing against mine. "Then we'll face it," she said simply.

Her confidence was infectious, and I found myself nodding. The weight of everything we'd faced—the rift, Abernathy, the Chronarium—felt lighter when she was beside me.

But as we left the ruins of the observatory, stepping into the quiet stillness of the night, I couldn't shake the feeling that the rift had left something behind—something we couldn't yet see.

The breeze carried the scent of ash and earth, the distant hum of insects breaking the silence. The world felt fragile like it wasn't quite done settling after what we'd just done. And yet, for the first time, I felt like I could breathe.

The carriage ride back was a blur. She'd shattered my world, the carefully constructed fortress of logic and precision I'd built around myself. And in its place, she'd built something new, something infinitely more complex and beautiful. She'd shown me the man I could be, the man hidden beneath the layers of metal and gears.

We reached my home, miraculously intact amidst the surrounding devastation. Evelyn walked ahead of me, her silhouette bathed in the moon's ethereal glow. All I could see was her, the way the moonlight outlined her profile, the way her hair caught the breeze. She'd pulled me from the endless cycle of machines and calculations, past the insecurities that had always held me captive, and shown me what it meant to be whole.

Evelyn walked ahead of me, her silhouette outlined by the moon's faint glow. She'd changed everything, not just the way I saw the world, but the way I saw myself. She'd pulled me out of my endless cycle of machines and calculations, past my insecurities, and made me feel whole.

I slowed my steps, my gaze lingering on her. Something else was on my mind, something I'd been holding back for too long. After everything we'd been through, I knew it was time.

"Evelyn," I called softly, my voice breaking the stillness.

She stopped and turned, her brow furrowing slightly as if she'd sensed the shift in my tone. "What is it?"

I hesitated, the words catching in my throat. But then she stepped closer, her eyes searched mine, and the rest of the world seemed to fade away.

"I…" I started, then shook my head with a soft laugh. "You make this harder than it should be, you know that?"

Her lips curved into a faint smile. "Good. Keeps you on your toes." But her teasing faded as she stepped closer, her expression softening. "What's on your mind, Thaddeus?"

I took her hand, the cool metal of my prosthetic brushing against her skin. "I've spent so much of my life building things, fixing things, but you've made me realize I can't fix everything. Least of all myself."

She opened her mouth to speak, but I gently shook my head. "Let me finish," I said, my voice quieter now. "You've done something no one else ever has. You've made me believe that maybe… maybe I don't have to be perfect to be enough."

Her eyes softened, and in that moment, I saw the walls she'd kept up begin to crack.

"You've been enough since the moment I met you," she said, her voice trembling slightly. "I just wish you could see that."

The words hit something deep inside me, and before I could second-guess myself, I pulled her closer. She didn't hesitate, her arms wrapping around me as I held her tightly, like letting go would shatter the fragile calm we'd found in this moment.

The world around us was broken, but here, in her arms, it didn't matter. Nothing else mattered.

"I don't want to put this off anymore," I murmured, my voice barely audible.

Her breath caught, and she pulled back just enough to look at me. Her gaze searched mine, and I could see the flicker of hesitation there—uncertainty, not in me, but in herself. But then she nodded, a faint smile tugging at her lips.

"Neither do I," she said softly.

The words hung between us for a moment, and then we were moving—together, instinctively, like the rest of the world had disappeared.

CHAPTER 21

$\mathcal{E}$velyn

And neither did I—at least not in that moment. Instead of answering, I stepped closer, my hands brushing against his chest, feeling the warmth radiating through the fabric of his shirt. The look in his eyes made my breath catch, a mixture of certainty and hunger, like he'd been holding himself back for far too long.

It was like a dam breaking. His hand slid to my waist, pulling me closer, and the strength in his grip sent a thrill coursing through me. My breath hitched, and for a moment, I could only stare up at him, my heart pounding so hard it felt like it might burst.

"Evelyn..." he murmured, his voice low, rough, and thick with restraint.

I didn't let him finish. I rose onto my toes, my hands curling into his shirt, and kissed him. It wasn't tentative or careful—it was everything I'd been holding back since the moment I met him. He made a sound deep in his chest, almost a growl, and then his arms were around me, lifting me off the ground like I weighed nothing.

I gasped against his lips, my hands tangling in his hair, and he didn't hesitate. The kiss deepened, his tongue sliding against mine, and I melted into him, clinging to his broad shoulders as he carried me. I didn't even realize we were moving until my back pressed against the doorframe of his room.

He paused there for a heartbeat, his breath ragged against my lips. "If this is too fast..."

"It's not," I said, cutting him off. My voice trembled, but it was steady where it mattered most. "I need you, Thaddeus. Please."

That was all it took. He kissed me again, harder this time, his lips trailing down my jaw to the curve of my neck. I tilted my head back, gasping as his teeth grazed my skin, and I felt the low rumble in his chest as he buried his face against my throat.

The door swung open behind me, and he carried

me inside, kicking it shut with a force that rattled the frame. He set me down, but his hands never left me, sliding to my waist and hips, pulling me flush against him.

"You drive me mad, Evelyn," he murmured, his voice a mix of frustration and reverence. His forehead pressed against mine, his breath warm against my lips. "Do you know what you're doing to me?"

I smiled, though my heart raced. "I think I have an idea."

His laugh was low and breathless, but it faded quickly as his hands moved again, his fingers brushing against the hem of my shirt. "May I?"

"Yes," I whispered, my voice barely audible.

He lifted the fabric slowly, his fingertips grazing my skin as he pulled it over my head. The room's cool air made me shiver, but his hands were there, warm and steady, sliding over my shoulders and down my arms until I felt like I might burn under his touch.

His gaze roamed over me, and the way he looked at me—like I was something precious, something he couldn't quite believe was real—made my cheeks flush.

"You're perfect," he said, his voice rough with emotion.

I laughed softly, nervously. "I'm not."

"You are to me," he said, and the conviction in his voice silenced any protest I might have made.

He kissed me again, slower this time, his lips exploring mine like he was memorizing me. My hands fumbled with his shirt, and he helped me, pulling it over his head in one smooth motion. My fingers traced the scars on his chest, the connection points where his prosthetic arm met his shoulder, and I felt him shudder under my touch.

"You're beautiful," I said, the words escaping before I could stop them.

He froze, his eyes meeting mine, and I saw the flicker of disbelief there. "No one's ever said that to me before."

Something in his expression shifted, and he kissed me again, deeper this time, his hands sliding down to the waist. He hesitated, his fingers curling into the fabric. "Are you sure?"

"Yes," I said, my voice steady now. "I've never been more sure."

He removed the rest of my clothing slowly, reverently, and I let him, my heart racing as I stood there, bare and exposed in every sense of the word. But when his eyes met mine, there was no judgment, no hesitation, only awe.

"You're incredible," he murmured, his hand brushing against my waist.

I reached for him, tugging at the waistband of his pants, and he didn't stop me. When he stood before me as bare and vulnerable as I was, I felt a flicker of nervousness. He was taller, broader, and stronger than I'd imagined, yet he looked at me like I had all the power.

"Thaddeus," I whispered, my hands sliding to his chest. "I want you."

"You have me," he said, his voice trembling. "All of me."

When he lowered me onto the bed, his movements were slow and calculated, as if giving me time to change my mind. But I didn't. I trusted him with everything I had, and when he finally joined me, it was like the world around us disappeared.

The first touch was a mix of newness and intensity, and I gasped, my hands gripping his shoulders as he moved with me. He paused, his forehead pressing against mine.

"Are you okay?" he asked softly, his voice thick with restraint.

"Yes," I said, my voice barely audible. "Don't stop."

He nodded, his movements slow and measured, my body coming alive as he touched me. His hands between my legs, circling the tight nub of nerves at the start of my slit sent me gasping for more before shuddering as a small orgasm tore through me.

"I want more," I whispered, out of breath.

He pushed my legs farther apart, the weight of his body both exhilarating and terrifying. The pressure of his cock at my entrance made me tremble, a mixture of anticipation and apprehension swirling within me. He paused, then slowly, gently eased himself in. A sharp sting shot through me, followed by a warmth that spread through my core. It was a new sensation, intense and unfamiliar, but the discomfort quickly faded, replaced by a burgeoning desire. My muscles adjusted to this thickness, welcoming him with a tight grip, then he pulled backward, momentarily leaving me wanting before plunging deep within me again. Moans of pleasure escaped my lips. It was overwhelming, but in the best way, like every nerve in my body was coming alive all at once.

His hands never stopped moving, caressing, reassuring, and every time I made a sound—every gasp, every moan—he responded, his touch growing surer, his pace quickening.

When the tension finally broke, it was like everything inside me shattered and reformed all at once, leaving me breathless and trembling in his arms. He held me through it, his lips brushing against my temple, murmuring my name like it was the only word he knew.

When it was over, he stayed close, his arms wrapped around me, his breath warm against my skin. I rested my head against his chest, listening to the steady rhythm of his heartbeat.

"I love you," I whispered, the words escaping before I could stop them.

His arms tightened around me, and he pressed a kiss to my hair. "I love you, too," he said, his voice soft and certain.

And I knew, in that moment, that I was exactly where I was meant to be.

EPILOGUE

$\mathcal{E}$velyn

The mansion was quiet now, the workshop ruins bathed in the soft orange glow of the setting sun. The air smelled of ash and rain, the remnants of the storm that had passed, but the chaos was truly gone for the first time in days. The rift was closed. Abernathy was gone, or at least we assumed, and, well, I had finally made love with Thaddeus. I would've stayed in his arms forever, but life pulled us out of his bed to dress and to inspect his workshop.

And yet, as we walked up the crumbling steps to the remains of Thaddeus's workshop, I couldn't shake the feeling that we were standing on the edge of something—not just an ending, but a beginning.

Clara stood in the doorway, her face pale and drawn, but her eyes lit up the moment she saw us. "You're alive," she breathed, her voice trembling with relief.

"Barely," I said, managing a weak smile.

She ran forward, throwing her arms around Thaddeus first, then me. For a moment, the three of us stood there, holding on to each other like survivors of a storm.

"You did it," Clara said, stepping back to look at Thaddeus. "You stopped him."

He nodded, his expression tired but calm. "The rift is gone. The Chronarium… it's destroyed."

Clara's gaze flicked to me, her brow furrowing. "And you?" she asked softly. "Are you staying?"

The question hit me like a punch to the chest. I'd been avoiding it, burying it beneath the urgency of survival and the chaos of the rift. But now, with the danger behind us, it was unavoidable.

I glanced at Thaddeus. He was watching me carefully, his blue eyes filled with something raw and unspoken.

"I am," I admitted, my voice barely above a whisper. "I have to, t. The pendant is destroyed." That had been my sacrifice, the most powerful thing I could set my intent on to ensure the pendant was at its most powerful to close the rift and stop Abernathy.

The truth was, I didn't belong there. It wasn't my time, my world. I was a survivor, someone who had always relied on keeping one foot out the door. I didn't know how to stay, not in one place, not with one person.

But as I looked at Thaddeus, something shifted inside me.

He turned away, walking into the wreckage of his workshop. The space was barely recognizable. Machines were overturned, tools scattered, and everything was coated in a layer of soot and debris. He stopped near the workbench, his metal hand brushing against the edge of a shattered device.

"I know it's not much..." he said, his voice low, "... but this is all I have. This place, this work. It's not a life. Not really."

I stepped closer, the floor creaking beneath my boots. "You think I care about that?"

He let out a sharp breath, shaking his head. "You should. You don't belong here, Evelyn. You have a whole world waiting for you. A future."

"And what if I don't want it?" I said, my voice rising. "What if I want this? You?"

He turned to face me, his expression twisted with doubt. "I'm not... whole, Evelyn. I've spent my life trying to fix things... machines, people, timelines. But I can't fix myself. I don't even know if there's anything left to fix."

I stepped closer, reaching up to cup his face. His skin was warm beneath my fingers, his stubble rough against my palm. "You don't need fixing," I said softly. "You're not broken, Thaddeus. You're human. And in case you haven't noticed, I'm not exactly perfect either."

He stared at me, his throat working as if trying to find the words. "Are you sure?" he finally asked, his voice barely audible.

I smiled, brushing my thumb across his cheek. "I've never been more sure of anything in my life."

For a moment, the world seemed to stop. Then his arms were around me, pulling me close, and I felt the tension in my chest ease. This was it. This was home.

Later, as the sun dipped below the horizon, we stood outside the mansion, watching the sky shift from orange to deep purple. The wind stirred faintly, carrying the scent of ash and earth. The mansion's ruins cast long shadows across the over-grown courtyard, the last light of the sun catching on broken glass and twisted metal.

"What happens now?" I asked, breaking the silence.

Thaddeus glanced at me, a faint smile tugging at his lips. "We rebuild," he said simply.

I nodded, but my mind was already spinning with possibilities. The rift was gone, but the world wasn't safe yet. There were still questions to answer and mysteries to solve. And for the first time, I wasn't afraid of the uncertainty.

As I turned, my foot caught on something in the dirt. I bent down, brushing away the debris, and froze.

It was a shard of the pendant, no larger than my palm. Its surface was cracked and scorched, but as I held it up to the fading light, a faint glow pulsed from within, soft and rhythmic, like a heartbeat.

"Thaddeus," I said, my voice tinged with unease.

He looked down at the shard, his expression darkening. "It shouldn't still be active."

"Do you think…" I trailed off, not sure how to finish the sentence.

He met my gaze, his jaw tightening. "I don't know. But whatever it is, we can handle it."

I slipped the shard into my pocket. The weight of it was comforting, a reminder of everything we'd fought for and everything we still had to fight for, and what I had given up.

As we turned back toward the mansion, I felt a

strange sense of calm. The future was uncertain, but for the first time, I wasn't running from it.

The End

Check out more books by Lilliana Rose

The Biologist and the Selkie

Moonlit Promenade: A beastly courtship
November 2025

The Encantado's Kiss

Claimed by the Incubus

The Green Man

Bk1: Dark Moon Secrets
Witch Moon Series

Bk1: Shadow Wolf
Protector Wolf Shifter Series

Dragon Bond: Part One
Dragon Reborn: Part Two

Enjoy academy books?
Check out the complete series of
Lost Souls Academy
Bk1: The Waking of Ghosts

Like to read different genres?
Check out Lilliana Rose's cowboy books
Chasing Dust Clouds
A Dusty Christmas
Best in Show
A Country Christmas
The Royal Show Affair
A Farmer's Christmas

Keep up with Lilliana Rose's new releases by joining
her newsletter.
https://landing.mailerlite.com/webforms/landing/
g9l7p6

ACKNOWLEDGMENTS

A huge thank you to Kaylene, Lisa, and Nikki for their expert eyes and editing skills in getting my story ready for publication. To Kit, thank you for another wonderful cover – you've captured the essence of the story perfectly! And of course, endless cuddles and a big, slobbery thank you to my furry writing assistant, Sprinkles, who keeps me company, reminds me to take breaks.

ABOUT THE AUTHOR

Lilliana Rose weaves enchanting tales of shifters, witches, and the monsters that lurk in the shadows of the unknown. Love ignites amidst the untamed wilderness, where ancient lore and cryptic prophecies whisper secrets of the past. When she's not conjuring thrilling plots, a quiet evening finds her curled up with a cup of tea (or a glass of red wine) and a book featuring a wolf or dragon on the cover. Lilliana brings a unique blend of logic and imagination to her writing, creating stories that will haunt your dreams and keep you spellbound until the very last page.